Lost Son of Salem: An American Boy's Odyssey in the Arab World

Mohammad AlFares

Published by Mohammad AlFares, 2024.

LOST SON OF SALEM: AN AMERICAN BOY'S ODYSSEY IN THE ARAB WORLD

First edition. May 10, 2024.

Copyright © 2024 Mohammad AlFares.

ISBN: 979-8224666744

Written by Mohammad AlFares.

To all the mothers of the world

Acknowledgements

I would like to express my gratitude to Abdullah Alfares and Salah Alshammary for their encouragement while reading the original manuscript. I also extend my thanks to my translator, Lucinda Wills, for the long hours she dedicated to making this translation possible. Special appreciation goes to my editor, Doreen Martens, for her meticulous work and insightful feedback.

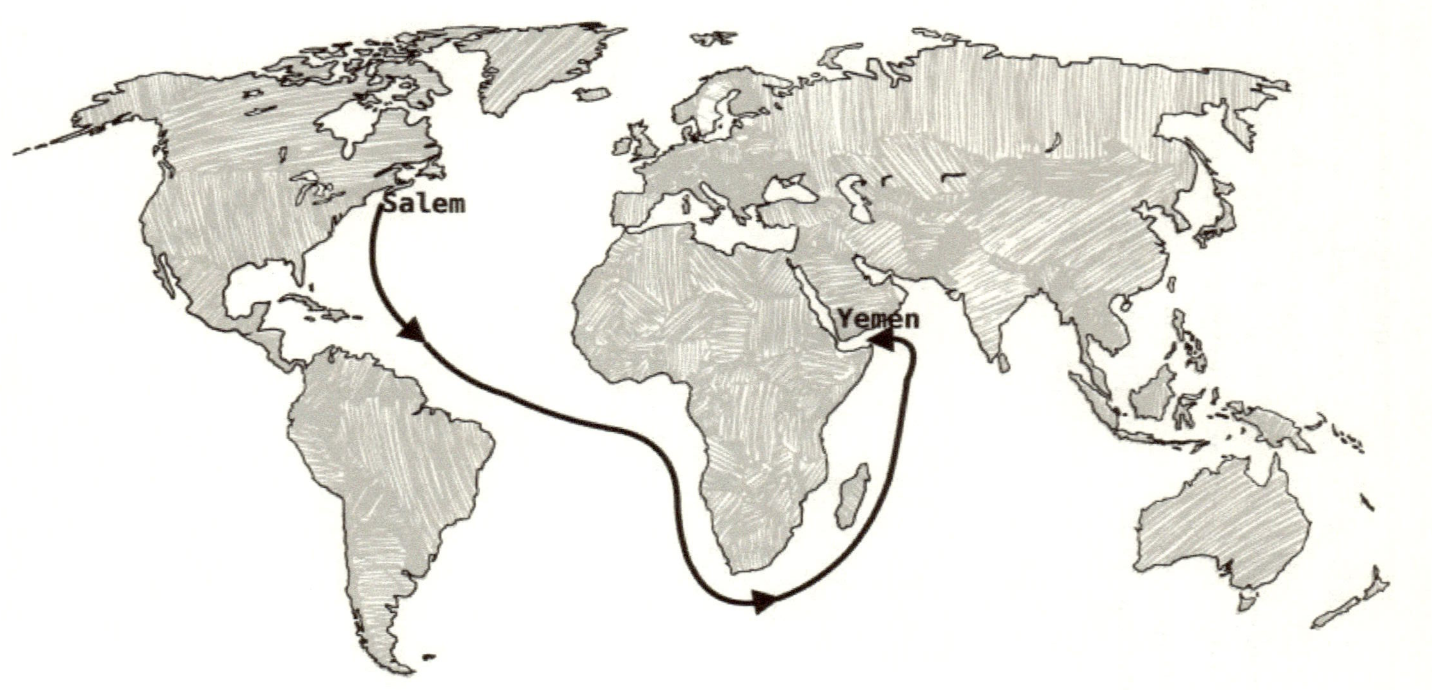

Salem
Yemen

Chapter One

Time: April 2013

Place: Big Sur, California

On a lofty bluff above the vast, sparkling ocean clings a rustic house. The rushing sound of waves dancing on the shore in effortless harmony wafts uninhibited into its open windows. The house is separated from the water only by the Pacific Coast Highway, which at this early hour is empty of cars and passersby except for a few joggers. In the afternoon, the road will teem with vehicles and bicycles of every kind and color, but for now a thick, silent fog shrouds the hill, the pitter-pat of light rainfall adding to a feeling of cozy comfort within the house. Tom's cell phone rings—an unwelcome sound at this hour.

Tom turns over in bed, hoping the ringing will stop, but it doesn't. He pushes the phone away until it drops off the nightstand, but it keeps on ringing. Grudgingly, he picks it up and slowly answers.

"Hello?" he asks gruffly.

"I'm sorry, sir. I hope I'm not disturbing you," says a woman at the other end.

"Disturbing me! It's 6 a.m., for God's sake!" he growls, barely able to open his eyes to see the clock hanging on his bedroom wall.

"I'm sorry ... I forgot the time difference between here and California. I'm calling from Salem, on the East Coast. It's 9 a.m. here."

"It's Saturday ... the weekend!" says Tom, slowly pulling his thoughts together.

"We haven't stopped working since we were hit by the storm."

Tom's memory is jolted to the news of the hurricane that hit the eastern seaboard. News coverage over the past two weeks has been non-stop. He usually cuts a call short as soon as he senses a solicitation, but something makes him stay on the line this time.

"So, what do you want?" Tom asks, yawning.

"I would first like to make sure that you are Thomas Paul. Do I have that right?"

"Who wants to know?"

"Sorry, I forgot to introduce myself. I'm Leslie Clark of the Federal Emergency Management Agency, FEMA. But before I explain the reason for my call, I have to check ... do you have any relatives in Salem, Massachusetts?"

"What? No ... no, I don't know anyone there."

"Are you sure?"

"Uh ... yes."

"All right, then. Maybe you're not the person we are looking for. I'm very sorry to bother you."

"Wait—" Tom says, slowly realizing something.

The sound of rain on the patio outside intensifies. Chasing a vague memory from childhood, Tom recalls his mother telling him his father had a great-great-uncle who lived in Massachusetts. That was a long time ago. A very long time.

"Yes?"

"Oh, it's nothing. I was thinking that maybe a relative lived on the East Coast, but that was a long time ago. It probably wouldn't concern you now."

"About how long ago?"

"I don't know ... probably more than a hundred years," he says, now ready to end the call and go back to sleep.

"Could I ask his name and birthplace and some other questions about your family history?"

"You can, but I'm not sure you'll get a proper answer from me now."
He hangs up and is soon back asleep.

At 9 a.m., Tom is sitting on the rocking chair on the patio, enjoying
the gentle April breeze and expansive view. The rain has stopped and
the sun is peeking through clouds that are looking lighter now. He
contemplates the hazy, distant horizon and wonders idly what might
happen to those fated to go out to sea when they reach that liminal
space where earth meets sky, one blending into the other.

His dog fetches the newspaper from the doorstep for him to read
as he sips his carefully prepared coffee. Tom owns a coffee shop, a
popular stop for tourists cruising the scenic Pacific Coast Highway. He
spends most of his time there, but on the weekends he escapes work to
spend time in this bucolic place he inherited from his father. The phone
rings again, and this time Leslie leads with the reason for her call. She
reminds him of the storm and the damage it caused to a lot of property.
No deaths, fortunately, but some injuries.

"But what does all this have to do with me?"

"The damage extended beyond buildings. It also struck some
graveyards, including one in the town of Salem. The rising water level
brought some coffins to the surface. We were able to return all the
coffins to their places quite quickly, except one."

Tom wonders impatiently where this tedious conversation is
heading.

"We opened the coffin in order to fix the lid and found a wooden
box inside, wrapped in a tattered cloth. It's possibly of historical
importance. The FEMA people didn't know how to handle such a case.
Should we return the box to the coffin or keep it out and return the
coffin to the ground? After conferring with FEMA's legal division, we
decided to search for living relatives of the person in the grave and hand
the box over to either them or the city's museum."

"Okay, so how does this relate to me?"

"The person in the grave is a woman with your family's surname."

"There are hundreds, probably thousands of people with the same last name," Tom interjects.

"That is true, but thanks to some genealogy websites, we were able to exclude most of them very quickly, narrowing down the possible relatives to three people. Two of them, I believe, are your cousins living in Santa Barbara, Kyle and Mark."

"Yes, I know Kyle and Mark—"

"At first they were interested, but later they changed their minds. I think they expected to receive an inheritance from someone who died recently, but when they learned it was just a box we would hand over to them, they pulled out. Anyway, you're the only person we can give the box to, because legally it belongs to you and we are obligated to inform you of it."

"So why don't you just send it to me?"

"We can't do that. City law requires attendance in person. Listen, Tom, I have spent much more time on this matter than I should have. Frankly, there are a lot of living people I should be helping instead of wasting my time with this. We will give you three days. Then we'll have to hand over the items we found in the coffin to the museum and they'll become state property."

"Hmm, okay. I need an address in case I decide to come," he says indifferently.

Leslie gives him her office address in Salem, doubtful she's even convinced him of the story. Before hanging up, she asks, "You work in coffee, right? ... Was that inherited?"

"What do you mean?"

"Did you know that the people of Salem used to trade in coffee long ago, back when it was still a precious product? Maybe you'll find something of interest to you here. Goodbye."

Tom doesn't take a lot of time to think it over. He's been looking for an excuse for a short vacation after weeks of non-stop work anyway, and he'd already been thinking of a trip to New England. He calls his

assistant to let him know he'll be gone for a week. *It'll be an adventure,
he thinks, and who knows? Maybe I'll discover an heirloom or two
handed down by some distant ancestor.*

He has no difficulty reserving a seat on a flight to Boston the next
day. Through the five-hour flight, he alternates between wondering
what's in the mysterious box and second-guessing his compulsion to
find out. He reminds himself that he's really here because he was
overdue for a vacation, and it was only coincidence that he took a
phone call from FEMA about something that happened to be near his
intended itinerary through New Hampshire, Maine, and Vermont.

On arrival at Logan Airport, Tom rents a car and heads towards
Salem, no more than twenty miles away. He goes directly to the address
that Leslie gave him on Lafayette Street.

He hadn't given her any reason to expect him, but she looks happy
to see him. After he signs off on some forms, she hands him the box,
wrapped in a plastic bag, which he takes back to the small hotel where
he plans to spend the night. He places the box on the nightstand and
goes out to get some dinner.

Though worn out from travelling, on his return he can't resist the
impulse to open the package he has travelled across the continent to
collect. He takes from the bag the mysterious box, carefully releasing
it from the tattered piece of cotton broadcloth in which unknown
hands wrapped it long ago. The box is plain, wooden, with rusty hinges
that, with a little force, open to reveal the contents: a book, with many
yellowed vellum pages and a leather cover. He opens it gingerly and
tries to read the words, but they're not in English. He opens an app on
his phone to check the unfamiliar script and determines that it is, as he
suspected, Arabic. A bit overwhelmed, he closes the book and goes to
bed.

In the morning, after a rushed breakfast, he searches his browser
for a local Arabic translator—not an easy task in a small town. After
finding a freelancer willing to take on the job in Boston, he heads

back to the city. The drive gives him time to think about the potential historical value of the little tome, and he stops off at an office supply store to make a careful photocopy to give the translator. He'll keep the original with him, he decides.

Tom spends his vacation hopping from one New England state to the next, and finally returns to Boston to collect the completed translation.

Some of the pages were actually in antique English handwriting, not Arabic, the translator points out, which indicates there were two or possibly more writers. He tells him, with a bemused look, that this was a particularly absorbing assignment. But Tom, busy handing over his credit card to pay, doesn't take the time to ask why; he's already late for his plane.

Back at Logan, though, Tom discovers that his flight to L.A. has been delayed a couple of hours, so he heads for the Starbucks in the departure lounge, orders a mocha, and finds a secluded spot to relax. The airport monitors are soundlessly replaying the same boring political coverage as always, making the contents of his carry-on bag a more enticing prospect.

He stretches his legs out to the low table in front of him and pulls the translated pages from his bag. As he leafs through the manuscript, he realizes the translations from Arabic have been interspersed with short narratives in English, apparently composed by a different hand. He begins to read, letting his imagination fill in the details that passing time has blurred.

TIME: 1805

Place: Salem, Massachusetts

It is autumn in Salem, a famous port in the fledgling United States of America. Thomas Jefferson is serving as the third president of the united former British colonies. In many ways, this place is the fruit of the age of exploration that began in the fifteenth century, notably with Portuguese navigators and then the Spanish, both seeking alternative routes to Asia. Their impetus was a quest to expand trading, particularly in the spices coveted for their use in preserving and enhancing food. For centuries, Arab traders transported many of the desired goods from the Middle East, India and the Far East to the eastern coasts of the Mediterranean, from which ships from Genoa and Venice carried the goods into the heart of Europe.

European rulers sought to circumvent Muslim control of eastern trade routes and commenced sea campaigns with the dual purpose of exploration and discovery and spreading Christianity. As the Portuguese-Spanish hegemony over such trade waned, competition emerged between the English and the French to control land and sea territories and extend their influence by way of colonization, particularly in North America. By the eighteenth century, a wave of European emigration to the New World had led to the creation of the thirteen British colonies that would come to constitute the original core of the United States.

In one of those colonies, John Herman Paul was born, which is where this story is set in motion.

YOUNG BOYS LAUGH AS they race across the wharf, unencumbered by adult worries, as grizzled longshoremen unload a sailing ship's goods onto the pier, lifting heavy crates onto their backs to deliver them to carts for transport. Mounds of sacks filled with coffee beans are piled next to stacked boxes of tea. Other crates redolent of nutmeg, cloves, and black pepper send their aromatic scents into the air, filling the October breeze with a teasing hint of their exotic origins.

One of the boys jumps into a small cart he has made for himself, and his pal pushes him under a horse-drawn cart; he manages to reach the other side and double back again, inciting shouts from the laborers to stay away and not hamper their work. Another boy sits proudly in his own cart, on which he has erected a wooden mast and spread across it a sail made of an old patched-up shirt. Sitting there, he imagines himself to be sailing on the high seas, the winds of adventure propelling him to hitherto unknown shores. Gusts and a spirit of exploration transport him to lands no one has heard of, to meet people the likes of whom no one has seen—perhaps the strangers his mother tells him about at bedtime.

His imagination lingering in distant times and places, the boy is oblivious to the calls of his friend, trying to warn him of the huge merchandise cart about to collide with him. Swiftly rolling his make-believe ship, he remains engrossed in his reverie. Suddenly, a man's hand reaches out and grabs the little boy, deftly pulling him from danger just before the overloaded cart crashes into him.

"You should pay more attention, son," the man says to the boy, whose nerves have been shaken by this near accident. Panting from fright, the boy notes that the man doesn't look like the rough working men at the port. He wears a finely tailored vest over a dazzling white linen shirt, topped by an elegant overcoat. Everything about his bearing and manner of dress indicate a man of affluence.

"What's your name, son?" the man asks, keeping one eye on the ships that have appeared on the horizon, headed for the port—eight in all, he noted moments ago.

"John ... John Herman Paul. I didn't mean to hurt anyone, sir," says the boy, his voice shaking.

"It's all right, John. Don't forget to take your shirt. As for your tiny ship, I'm afraid there's nothing left of it after that merchandise cart ran over it."

The man goes on his way, leaving John to gaze sorrowfully at the scattered bits of wood trampled under horses' hooves, as if his dreams have evaporated with the obliteration of his ship on the wharf. His friend Henry, who had been watching this brief encounter closely, rushes toward him, reminding him that he warned him of the impending danger. As usual, John had drifted into daydreams when he got into that little cart.

"Do you know who that was?" Henry asks about the man who rescued him. John shakes his head no. "That was William Orne, the trader. His family is famous in Salem. He owns the coffee trading store in Essex County."

As the sun sets, the two boys race each other home, passing the port warehouses and the grand three-story home facing the sea built by the Derby clan and now occupied by the Hawkes family. When they part, John begs his friend to not tell his father about the cart accident, making him swear on it. If they heard of it, his parents would no doubt forbid him from going to the wharf and watching the ships coming in to dock. John arrives to find his father fixing a broken kitchen window near the front door. He sneaks in through the back door and goes quietly up to his attic room to avoid being questioned about his tardiness.

Having dutifully washed his hands, he joins the family at the table, dinner preceded as always by giving thanks to the Lord for His bounty. John's family descends from English settlers who sailed from Holland to New England between 1620 and 1640 and settled in the Massachusetts colony, bringing with them their Puritan version of Protestantism. His father, Herman, chats with his wife, Faith, sharing news heard about town. Today he mentions the ships returning from the southern Arabian Peninsula and the profits being made by their traders. John listens attentively. This is the first time the word "Arab" has fallen on his ears. He knows a little about China and India, but he had not yet heard of the Arabs.

At bedtime, as usual, John asks his mother to tell him a story. This time, she tells him about the supposed witches who lived in Salem a century ago, before the founding of the country. Innocent people were put on trial amid mass hysteria about witchcraft all around Salem. It is a hair-raising story indeed, but John prefers her other tales about pirates on the high seas, and the merchants who sail to utopias in far-off lands. Faith is a wonderful teller of stories, which she narrates in a hushed voice that makes him feel as if he is meeting the people in her story face to face.

John's eyes begin to droop as night falls over the houses facing the sea, announcing the end of the busy work day in what has become the sixth largest city in the United States. Its daily economy is mostly devoted to fishing, but Salem is also famous for its skilled seamen and navigators, often privateers, who not long ago played a prominent role in the revolutionary war against the King by storming and seizing British ships.

The town's markets open their doors early in the morning, displaying myriad wares to their customers. Among the row of shops is a warehouse established by Captain Henry Prince, from which he sells goods from the West Indies and all over the world: finely crafted tea and coffee cups made of Chinese porcelain; Russian fabrics; Turkish silk; Indian cotton; and most prized of all, spices such as Ceylon and Cochin cinnamon and black pepper from Sumatra—the most sought-after and expensive. The streets begin to abound with passersby, their faces reflecting a broad spectrum of peoples and occupations. There are storeowners, traders, and customs workers at the port; sailors and craftsmen such as carpenters and iron workers, shipbuilders, fishermen. And dark-skinned, enslaved men and women. All on their way somewhere, seeking their daily bread. This diverse population reflects Salem's role as a major stop on the emerging trade routes connecting Europe with China and India, whose seamen form a human link between the city and the four corners of the earth. Carved above the entrance of the Salem Customs House is the slogan, "To the Farthest Ports of the Rich East."

About a quarter of a mile from the port is a small building belonging to William Orne, whose family business includes about forty ships, all highest-quality commercial vessels, listed on the records of the state's ship registration department. The coffee in a cup on Orne's desks shimmers with the rumble of horse-drawn carriages passing by as he reviews some calculations. He pauses to glance at his pocket watch, in anticipation of the nephew he is expecting at any moment. At a knock on the door, he responds, "Come in, Joseph."

"I'm not Joseph, sir ... I ... I'm Herman Paul."

"Oh, I thought you were my nephew, Joseph." *What could have delayed him?* Orne mutters to himself.

"Please come in, Mr. Paul. What can I do for you?"

He rises to shake the visitor's hand and offer him a cup of hot coffee, which he accepts gratefully.

"I heard that you are planning to send one of your ships to the Arabian Peninsula," Paul begins.

"Word moves fast in this town."

"I would like you to take on my son, John. He's a dreamer, I'm afraid. Keeps wandering away from school and can't be kept at a desk, no matter how often the schoolmaster raps his knuckles. His mother and I have nearly given up on his learning how to do figures or anything useful, really. Learning a trade would benefit the boy. As it is, he's much given to idle amusement, especially dallying around the wharves. He seems peculiarly drawn to the life of a sailor. He would certainly be of much help to you. He could clean decks and work in the galley—"

"John—you mean the lad playing foolishly on the wharf that I rescued from being crushed the other day? John Paul? That's your boy? How old is he?"

"Er, eleven years of age," Paul answers, startled by Orne's words and exaggerating his son's maturity just a little.

"I don't know, Mr. Paul. Your son is very young for the rigors of such a voyage. Also, I am not the one who decides such matters. Responsibility for hiring a crew belongs to my nephew, Captain Joseph Orne."

Orne takes a sip of his coffee and wonders how to gracefully see the man out. This venture to Arabia is a new and more perilous one for his company; mostly his ships ply the regular trade between the port of Salem and the West Indies, carrying lumber and dried codfish to the British colonies there and returning with molasses.

The office door squeaks as it opens, to reveal a young man in his mid-twenties, wearing a captain's uniform.

"I'm so sorry I'm late, Uncle," he announces, rather more loudly than necessary. "I was looking for a replacement for the cook's assistant, who has come down with a fever. I fear he won't be able to sail with us. Oh, I beg your pardon," he says, noticing Paul. "I didn't know you had a visitor."

"No, it's all right. Come in. Seems you came at the right time. The man sitting before you may have a solution for your present dilemma."

Paul's eyes glisten. "He could assist the cook. Yes, John is quite fond of kitchen work."

Orne introduces his nephew to his guest and explains the context for this exchange. On hearing the boy's age, Joseph Orne is hesitant, expressing his concern that the cook, a crusty old freedman named Leon, might not accept such a recruit. But he yields to the father's insistence, given that replacing the assistant is one of many urgent tasks yet to be tackled before the ship sails.

Reluctantly, he agrees to take Paul's son, but only after describing the hardships to come on the months-long journey at sea. They will probably not return before mid-year at least, he warns, probably later. Paul nods his head in comprehension of the trip's risks, expresses his gratitude to the captain, and leaves hastily before the captain has an opportunity to change his mind.

"Half a year," he mumbles to himself. "It will pass like a feather in the wind ... who knows, maybe John will return before I finish building the new stable." He puts far from mind the knowledge that winds may blow ships in undesirable directions, that passing days will reveal what was previously unknown, and news will come to the unprepared.

Joseph Orne removes the coffee cups from his uncle's big desk and rolls out the navigational maps he has brought with him, along with a copy of *The American Practical Navigator,* the book by the self-taught mathematician Nathaniel Bowditch, which was published three years ago but is already an indispensable guide for the sailors of his native Salem. He traces his finger over a map detailing the eastern coast of the great continent of Africa and pauses when his finger reaches the lower end of the Red Sea, on the western shore of Yemen. Here is Mokha, and to the north Luhayya, and Hudaydah just south.

With his uncle, he reviews the ports on the ship's itinerary, the quantity of merchandise they hope to purchase, the type of coffee, and the budget allocated for it all—an heretofore unimaginable sum of sixty thousand dollars, counted in cash from Orne's funds, that he will carry with him. The journey is motivated by his uncle's high hopes for even higher profits, having heard of the gains made by the eight ships that have anchored at Salem's port after voyages to Arabia Felix.

Orne's family controls scores of ships, some by direct ownership and some by having a family member as the captain. William also co-owns some ships with other traders and has a retinue of captains to man the helm. He has chosen his nephew Joseph for this voyage in spite of the doubts his assistant raised as to the young man's preparedness for such a difficult trip.

Faith doesn't need to do much to prepare for her son's travels, beyond suppressing her fears and tender emotions. Their standard of living is like that of most residents of Salem who feel compelled to send their boys out to sea, to fish or to work on commercial trading ships, in hopes of learning the skills to earn a proper living by the age of seventeen or eighteen. That his father would go looking for a suitable place for him at some point was inevitable, and John is instantly enthusiastic about the idea.

But he is a child, not even ten yet! Despite his disregard for school, he has a keen intellect and listens avidly to his mother's stories and to port workers' stories of lands beyond the sea. He has no idea of what is to come, other than his father's rosy description of a sea outing that will take him on a grand adventure for a few weeks or possibly months. When he returns, the father says, he will find the new stable completed and will be able to ride the pony he has been promised.

Herman Paul has no direct experience to bear on this choice, having spent his life working as a carpenter, his time on the sea limited to a few days on a ship to visit his sister to the south. The most difficult part of it is convincing his wife that John's travel would be for his own benefit. How does one persuade a mother to cast her only son upon the mercy of the sea, in the company of strangers!

"Missions make men!" he tells Faith, to which she replies, "Rather, mothers make men!"

The father lists the names of influential and famous figures in Salem, Roger Williams and Henry Prince and others, who were only boys when they first went to sea. He comforts mostly himself with this recollection, quietly fearing that his wife will succeed in changing his mind. "But ... but he is nine years old," she responds.

Though Faith has always anticipated the day when her son would depart on one of the ships moored in their harbor, she had not imagined it would be so soon. She wants nothing more than to keep her sweet boy in her embrace, and agreeing to allow John to take up the sailing life means agreeing to allow her heart to crumble on the day he goes aboard. Every day, John's father goes to William Orne's office to inquire about the departure date, and every day the answer is the same: when the winds are right.

The smell of cheap coffee wafts through the small house, even to the attic where John lies sleeping in his warm bed. Slowly opening his eyes, he finds his mother kneeling at the end of the bed in silent prayer. Seeing his devout mother in prayer is nothing new, but there is something unintelligible in her expression now, something staid and coldly resigned. She seems frozen in place, unaware that he is watching her. He closes his eyes again, pretending to sleep. He does not want her to know he saw her in such a state. Some time passes.

Suddenly, Faith gently shakes her son's shoulder to wake him. "John, John ... it's time."

Later, sitting together at the breakfast table, Herman Paul speaks of what remains to be done to prepare for the voyage and asks John if he has forgotten any of the items on the list. John shakes his head yes or no on each point. His mother says nothing.

It is said that a thousand-mile journey begins with a single step. Thousands of miles lie ahead on this voyage, and the first step begins with pain and sorrow pressing on a woman's heart. Faith tries to separate her heart from her body so she can bid him a proper farewell, but walks through the morning as if drugged. She watches her son lift his knapsack over his shoulder and go down the stairs. He has filled the knapsack with a few supplies, old clothing, and some puppets and toys his friend Henry gave him. Crumbs from his favorite biscuits, ones she made, leave a faint trail behind him. He stops at the bottom of the stairs to gingerly gather up the pieces dropped along the way, as if they were the scattered remnants of her broken heart. He lingers at the doorstep, waiting for his father to arrive from the stable, his mother gazing at him with desperate longing from the kitchen. Her lower lip trembles as if saying a prayer. Just a few steps separate them now, perhaps as close as she will ever be to him again, but her feet refuse to move toward a final goodbye.

Herman Paul calls from outside, interrupting this moment. Casting a last look towards his mother, John says goodbye and asks her to leave his bedroom door open in case he returns at night and does not want to wake her up. Their eyes meet for a moment, and the mother stretches out her arms just as John turns to step outside. He closes the door behind him, leaving her standing still, with outstretched arms.

"Closing the door behind you is the hardest part of a journey," his father says as he snaps the reins to send the open cart rattling through the streets of Salem on this wet and cloudy day. The trip down Chestnut Street takes them to Derby Wharf, where three huge warehouses receive imported goods. They are built three stories high, to prevent seawater from reaching the merchandise in a storm; the difference between low and high tides in Salem can be as much as fifteen feet. There are dozens of wharves at the port and Derby is the longest, reaching nearly half a mile in length.

The wharf's namesake, Elias Derby, is one of the most famous traders in Salem and owner of the well-known *Grand Turk*, the first New England vessel engaged in direct trade with China. Derby both supported and benefited from the American Revolution by using his ship as a privateer to capture dozens of English ships and integrate them into his commercial fleet.

Bit by bit, activity in the port pulls into full swing. Customs inspectors pass by the tall ships at the dock and observe those still coming in. A customs worker earns a dollar and a quarter a day for his work, which includes boarding incoming ships to inspect their cargo and determine their conformity with the laws of the new country. The customs tax collector and his notebook-bearing assistants make the rounds with surveyors responsible for weighing and measuring the goods heaped up on the wharves and in the warehouses and calculating the corresponding tax to be levied on the traders.

Uncharacteristically, John walks holding his father's hand and clinging to him, hardly detaching himself until they reach the end of the wharf. This is the same wharf he has visited so often, romping unhindered from corner to corner and gleefully playing with his friends. But today he approaches it somberly, without his usual enthusiasm. *Essex* rocks gently at the edge of the pier. Men purposefully walk up and down the gangway. Young Captain Orne emerges on deck and, spotting the pair, calls down to John. Releasing his tight grip on his son's hand, the father turns him over to the captain and implores him to treat John well. Herman Paul peers into the young captain's eyes and asks him if he believes in God.

"Of course," he replies.

"Then, I beseech you in the name of the good Lord to return my son to me in sound health, just as I have delivered him to you."

The captain gives him his word that he will not return unless his son is with him. Otherwise, he will never return. Joseph Orne speaks with confidence, as if he sees the future before his eyes, although he has no idea what fate has in store for him.

The father doesn't wait for the ship to depart. He has unfinished work waiting for him. But as he walks away, Herman Paul finds it difficult to take his eyes off his young boy he has now entrusted to the belly of that ship. When he finally returns home, he opens the door to find Faith frozen in the position she took at the moment she bid her son farewell, her arms still outstretched.

MOHAMMAD ALFARES

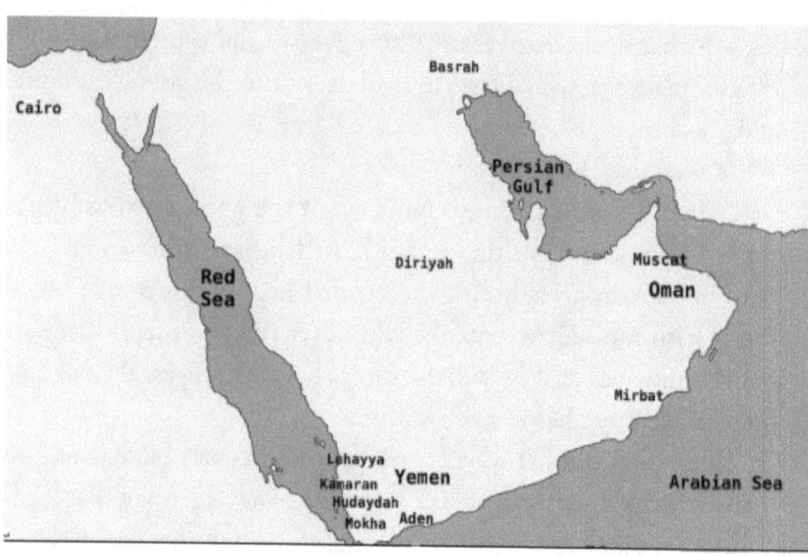

Chapter Two

On the other side of the earth live people whose culture could not be more different from that of the people of Salem. They speak another language, practice another faith, wear different clothing, inhabit houses strange to the eyes of anyone in Salem, and eat food unlike that found in New England. Yet they share the same emotions and human ambitions. They have the same hopes and aspirations and are driven by the same sentiments and instincts. They feel pain and joy like any other, experience hunger and satiety, toil and rest. They get angry and reconcile, they speak the truth and they lie, they fear and are reassured. They are brothers from the same origin, set apart perhaps by the degree of civilization attained by what the human mind had so far produced, but at the root connected by the most basic of human tendencies.

While the *Essex* departs from the port of Salem on the coast of the Atlantic Ocean, on the coast of the Red Sea, one Muhammad bin Aqeel is saying goodbye to his host, Al-Sharif Hamoud bin Muhammad, the ruler of Abu Arish, to return to the island he just purchased from his host. Closing the sale was the purpose of his visit.

A relative calm prevails over the Red Sea coast of the Arabian Peninsula following the fall of Makkah into the hands of Saud ibn Abdul Aziz, the grandson of Imam Muhammad ibn Saud, ruler of Al-Diriyah. The deposed Al-Sharif Ghalib seeks asylum in Jeddah, where he has conciliated Ibn Saud. Abu Nuqta, a shaykh of Asir, has ceased to attack the southern regions of the Red Sea adjacent to Hudaydah.

Thanks to this political calm in the region known as Hijaz, prices have dropped on various kinds of merchandise, and trade by sea is flourishing.

Over on the eastern Gulf coast of the Peninsula, however, there is political disarray. The weakness of the Arab Emirate of Bahrain has left a void exacerbated by the growing influence of the ruler of Al-Diriyah, aided by the Qasimis of Ras Al-Khaimah. This collides with the aspirations of the Sultan of Oman and his naval forces. At the same time, Britain is paying attention to the region as it casts a wary eye on Napoleon's ambitions to expand eastward to Iran and India.

Bin Aqeel sets out on his ship from the port of Luhayya with a crew composed of ordinary sailors and some slaves, threading west through an archipelago of small islands whose banks are protected by mangroves, before heading south. He appears content with the results of his difficult negotiations to purchase the island, talks that had come close to failing altogether.

Muhammad bin Aqeel Al-Saqqaf belongs to the Alawi line of Sayyids, descendants of the Prophet Muhammad, whose ancestors came from the Hijaz to settle in Dhofar, on the eastern side of the peninsula. His pursuit of trade has helped him amass a great fortune that brings with it power and authority, especially in the political void consuming Dhofar. Bin Aqeel owns a fleet of ships that trade in spices and wood from India. He has also traded in slaves, whom he puts to service on the ships, while favoring Frenchmen as captains and navigators for his vessels.

As they sail south, a servant alerts Bin Aqeel to another ship, sighted by a lookout up in the mast, that is tacking north. Soon, the mystery ship is visible from the deck, being escorted by a small British naval vessel. Bin Aqeel does not have good relations with the English and chooses to ignore the unknown ship, but he can't shake a creeping suspicion that its presence here does not bode well.

A few hundred yards away, on that other ship, a passenger, one Dr. Pringle, tells his companion of news he obtained from a private contact that Al-Sharif Hamoud intends to sell the island of Kamaran to Bin Aqeel. A relatively barren island, uninhabited save a few destitute fishermen, it has been the focus of rival powers' attention for years because of its central location at the lower end of the Red Sea, about nineteen miles southwest of Luhayya. Ships are cruising the Red Sea uncontended now, especially since Napoleon's armies evacuated Egypt. Kamaran seems a suitable location for the English to gather forces and construct a fortification there, but they missed the opportunity when they failed to utilize a royal directive they obtained from Sultan Selim III, the Ottoman caliph at the time, permitting them to use the island. Only about six years have passed since the French campaign in Egypt led by Napoleon Bonaparte, which aimed to block the route between Britain and its colonies in India, as well as exploit the country's resources to fund its campaigns and render Egypt the empire's eastern base. The English sided with the Ottomans against the French to oust them from Egypt, but France remains a force to be reckoned with for the English. Consequently, Dr. Pringle, a British acting administrator in the city of Mokha in Yemen, is outraged to learn of French intentions to found a colony on Kamaran.

Dr. Pringle's ship glides cautiously among the coral reefs until it drifts up to Antufash Island, where its naval escort vessel puts down anchor. From there, he continues his course east in the commissioned ship to Luhayyah, where mangrove trees rooted beneath the water's surface extend their upper branches like a green wall, protecting the city from easy invasion.

Pringle immediately takes a tender to the port with his assistant. He hurries briskly through the town, headed for Al-Sharif Hamoud's hilltop residence, his thoughts racing. The town appears prosperous, consisting mainly of baked mud-brick buildings and houses overlooking the sea, decorated with gypsum whitewash in elaborate relief motifs around the window and door frames, window arches, and parapets. The intricately carved wooden latticework *mashrabias*—bay windows holding clay water urns that allow the breeze to pass through while keeping the water cool—are of unparalleled beauty.

Snippets of Western languages pelt Pringle's ears on his way through the streets. This is where the Danish explorer Niebuhr stayed in 1764, writing extensively about what he saw and experienced. Indeed, a variety of foreign communities have lived, worked, and traded here for some time, enjoying a tolerant, urbane environment that accepts others and harbors no misgivings or suspicions towards the stranger.

At the peak of Qafl Mount, Al-Sharif Hamoud's residence sits grandly next to Al-Zailaee Mosque, with its three domes, on a well-fortified site that offers a view of all those entering and leaving the town. Pringle notices a lack of guards around the heights, not what he had expected from a person of such stature as Al-Sharif Hamoud. He introduces himself to the army commander as the British acting resident in Mokha and asks permission to meet Al-Sharif. That request granted, a soldier leads him upwards in the fort.

As they climb the stairs, his escort informs him that Al-Sharif Hamoud is not present, but he may meet his brother's son, Al-Sharif Yahya. Pringle's ascent is labored. He has lived much of his life on the sea and has never been interested in climbing mountains. Born into an aristocratic Yorkshire family from the north of England that had relocated to London, he studied Oriental languages before assuming posts under the foreign affairs office. In Bombay, he was responsible for collecting intelligence reports and employing local residents to serve the empire.

As they reach the last step at last, he stops to take in the view and catch his breath in the invigorating November breeze. Behind him are scattered other castles and fortifications on neighboring hilltops, and below is the sea, stretching as far as the eye can see. In between is Luhayya, walled on three sides. The city bustles with the coming and going of residents around its famous port, where ships bearing Yemeni coffee await their turn to depart or enter. Nothing blocks the transport of coffee beans, other than an archipelago of islands dotting the coral reefs, beyond which the ships seek out all corners of the earth. This is Arabia Felix, the happy Yemen.

Pringle quickly wraps up his initial courtesy meeting with Al-Sharif Yahya, then heads for one of the Indian traders living in Luhayya with whom he has had a longstanding friendship since his days in Bombay. There is no coastal city in this part of the Red Sea where Pringle does not have at least one informant. He strives to maintain the loyalty of those eyes, who do not even know each other, so that the credibility of their information can be assured.

The Indian trader confirms the news that Bin Aqeel has, in fact, closed a deal with Al-Sharif Hamoud to purchase Kamaran Island. The negotiations between Bin Aqeel and Al-Sharif were no secret—all the merchants had been talking about it some weeks before—but the talks did not come to fruition until just a few days ago.

To verify what he heard, Pringle goes with his escort to see the cannons and gunpowder that were part of the deal, which are now in the process of being moved from their storage site. He recognizes markings that indicate they indeed came from France.

Pringle returns to Al-Sharif Yahya to request a meeting with Al-Sharif Hamoud himself, since the nephew does not know enough about the nature or extent of the arrangements regarding the island and isn't authorized to speak on behalf of his uncle in any case. After much persistence on Pringle's part, Yahya agrees to accompany him on what will be a full-day trek to reach Wadi La'ah, a place north of Luhayya, a branch of the valley called Wadi Moor

They travel a whole day on camelback, and at last Pringle and his host, Al-Sharif Yahya, reach a large tent staked at the edge of the valley, surrounded by heavily armed soldiers. Under their wary gaze, Yahya leads him into the tent, where a slim man of medium height stands waiting for him, a sheathed sword hanging at his side and a dagger attached at an angle in the front of his belt, glistening in its silver sheath. Al-Sharif Hamoud's facial features are uncomplicated, lending him an unthreatening look, but the twinkle in his eyes suggests a sharp intellect. Pringle is put in mind of his favorite figure in Islamic history, Maawiya, who is said to have enlisted the people of Yemen, using the money of the people of the Levant, to fight the people of Iraq.

Al-Sharif Hamoud belongs to a lineage of Ashraf, also descendants of the Prophet Muhammad. Politics seem to have been his destiny, and he has acquired skills for maintaining regional equilibrium among various powers. Hamoud rules an area called Abu Arish in the Mikhlaf region and has a long history of clashes and compromises with the ruler of Asir, appointed by Ibn Saud, of the First Saudi State.

After formal greetings are exchanged, Pringle wastes no time getting to the point of his visit. Cool and composed, he explains his government's point of view, which is that Bin Aqeel purchased Kamaran Island only to lease it to the French—who, as soon as they get their hands on it, will build fortifications there that will pose a danger to British interests as well as the interests of local traders in that part of the Red Sea.

Pringle is aware that he is dealing with someone well known for his shrewdness and ability to prevaricate. For this reason, simple rejection or agreement are not the only possibilities.

Al-Sharif Hamoud is quite aware of the growing role of the English in the region but not comfortable with Pringle's assertions, especially since he has already received payment for the island. He doesn't want to give up the cannons, which he can use in his own expansion efforts and battles with enemies, but Pringle's doggedness makes him reconsider.

After first objecting, Al-Sharif goes on the defensive, saying he was not aware of Bin Aqeel's intention to lease the island to a foreign power.

Hearing a slight change in Al-Sharif Hamoud's tone, Pringle's eyes twinkle at the prospect that his visit will not be in vain after all, and that he might just succeed in aborting the deal. But just as he's beginning to think he's cinched it, Al-Sharif abruptly declares he cannot renege on a closed deal.

However, he suggests a compromise: he will send a letter to Bin Aqeel requesting him not to allow any type of foreign settlements or fortifications to be established on the island. Pringle accepts this halfway concession and is happy with his accomplishment. The two men return to Luhayya and exchange gifts to express their satisfaction with the results of their meeting.

Sailing back to Mokha, Pringle prepares a report to his government describing the French plan to establish a colony on Kamaran Island and his effort to thwart this plan by agreeing with Al-Sharif Hamoud to set conditions for his sale of the island.

Mokha is about a hundred and fifty miles south of Luhayya, at the entrance to the Red Sea, and only about forty-four miles from the strait of Bab Al Mandab. It acquired strategic importance in the days of Ottoman control over parts of the Arabian Peninsula. Ships would anchor in Mokha to pay a tax of passage to enter the Red Sea, but what has brought it immortal fame—a name that would still be associated with coffee many centuries later—is its port, from which cargo ships exported first-class Yemeni coffee beans.

Its name is enough to make a coffee shop owner proud when serving a special cup of mocha coffee to his customer, because he can be certain of its high quality. The best beans are like jewels picked from trees growing at elevations between three thousand and six thousand feet with a relatively warm and humid climate, as is the case in Yemen. Coffee, first cultivated and processed here, has spread to all inhabited places to become the most popular beverage in the world. At various times, coffee has also been subject to seizures and prohibitions. Because of its use in religious ceremonies among Sufis, it was prohibited by some other Muslims for a time, considered a substance for heretics. Murad IV of the Ottoman caliphate issued a decree forbidding coffee cultivation.

As Pringle is sending his report from Mokha to his superiors in Bombay, Bin Aqeel is busy constructing fortifications and transferring supplies to Kamaran in preparation for establishing a colony for his French customers. Bin Aqeel's relationship with the French goes back to the days when he would visit their colony in Mauritius in the Indian Ocean, where he owns some farmland. He has shared interests with some French naval officers who left the service to run private businesses or become privateers, turning a handsome profit by robbing British ships.

Kamaran is little more than 12 miles long from north to south, and only about four miles wide. Only a few miles separate it from the mainland, especially in the southern portion, where the water separating the two is only a little over a mile wide.

Al-Sharif Hamoud's letter reaches Bin Aqeel at his residence in Mokha, informing him of the new condition that he may not rent the island to any foreign party. Infuriated, Bin Aqeel cannot recall Al-Sharif laying down any conditions for purchasing the island during the negotiation. It is his property now, and he can handle it in any way he pleases, he reasons, especially because he had paid for it in advance. Pondering the matter after reading the letter, he is convinced that his suspicions about that mysterious ship encountered on his return trip were well-founded. He decides to return immediately to Luhayya to dissuade Al-Sharif Hamoud from this condition.

But he meets with a deaf ear. Al-Sharif refuses to budge.

In a small cabin at the stern of the ship anchored at the port of Salem, Captain Joseph Orne sits before a wooden desk and pulls the ship's diary from the desk drawer to make his first daily entry. This record will remain an important part of the ship's property, for future reference when needed. He dips his pen in a ceramic inkwell, pulls the ink up and starts to write.

At eight in the morning on this day, the sixth of November of the year 1805, we depart on Essex, *owned by Mr. William Orne, and set out for our destination of Mokha in the Yemen, on the southern end of the Arabian Peninsula, with our intent being to purchase coffee there. We will head south through the Atlantic Ocean, skirting the American coastline. Then we will cross the ocean eastward to the African coast and continue south to the Cape of Good Hope at the southernmost end of the African continent, before turning again northward to the Red Sea. May the Good Lord protect us!*

The *Essex* unfurls its sails to embark on the first mile after its sendoff from the port of Salem, a speck on the map of the sprawling and yet sparsely inhabited northeastern region of the United States. The ship faces a long voyage, but on board is a crew of some of the most skilled American seamen alive, captained by the youthful Joseph Orne. Most hail from Salem or nearby cities. A small boy named John Paul accompanies them. The captain still wonders to himself why he agreed to allow the boy to come with them. He recalls his uncle's last words to him: that if he wishes to travel lightly and quickly, he must rid himself of heavy loads, the foremost of which are envy and jealousy, followed by selfishness and fear.

With full sails, the ship answers the call of the wind. Sailors shout as they attend to their tasks on the deck. The *Essex* glides eastward at first, but once it passes by Marblehead, it turns to starboard and heads south, the direction it will maintain for many long weeks to come. It passes by Cat Island, which the people of Salem once used as a quarantine site. Then it advances toward the open arms of the ocean, where it disappears from view of the land, swallowed up by water as far as the eye can see. In a few hours, the head of a cape appears to starboard, a place where some of the first immigrants set foot on the pristine lands of what would be the United States.

Just a few short hours from the start of the journey, Cook Leon calls on the boy John to help him prepare a meal composed of potatoes, cheese and hardtack biscuits, and some dried fish with a little beer. The sailors not on watch finish their first meal and lie down in their bunks, exhausted from the work of the first day at sea. The odor of seamen's sweat mingles with the lingering reek of fish while John collects and washes the dishes left in the aftermath of the meal and returns them to their trunk in the kitchen.

Day turns to night, the first night in his life John has spent away from home—on the deck of a sailing ship, rolling disconcertingly on the swells of the mighty Atlantic. He remembers his mother, whom he left with arms outstretched, and his father, who could not take his eyes off him, and his pal Henry, whom he had played with on the wharves just a few days before. He longs for his warm bed and his mother's stories. Tears soak the hood of the coat his father gave him, which he now wraps closely around him to ward off the cold and try to sleep. His parents have promised he will return home in a few months at the most, but he cannot help but feel dread of the unknown and a cautious fear of what the days ahead will bring.

John spends the next few days vacillating between nausea and vomiting over the rail into a dizzying sea. The remedy Leon mixed for him to alleviate his seasickness hasn't helped. Days pass, excruciatingly slow. The pitch-black nights are cold, the days wet and wearying. Three weeks go by on the turbulent seas, waves pounding relentlessly against the ship. Near the end of a particularly stormy night, the ship repeatedly rises to the tip of a rebellious wave as if mounted on a wild horse, only to plunge into a whirlpool that sends pots and pans flying topsy-turvy across the kitchen.

John sobs in despair over his fate and fails to notice that his light body has become like a feather in the wind. Someone runs to him with a rope and ties him to the kitchen trunk to keep him from being flung around dangerously. John hears the captain shout out to a sailor. Daring a glance upward through an unsecured hatch, he sees a wave crash over it, sending a flood of salty water down into the galley. He is overwhelmed to glimpse a sail detached from the mast, sagging and flapping uselessly while sailors dash about, cutting ropes to avert complete disaster. He is vaguely aware of Leon's voice, droning prayers at his side with supplications to the good Lord to save their ship, to have mercy on the *Essex*. John tilts with the ship's deflection after is it freed of its burden and recovers its balance. The world spins around him and his head hangs forward as he falls into oblivion.

John awakes to a familiar sound, and he cannot believe his ears. He listens closely; yes, it's the cry of the seagulls he used to chase with his friends on the wharves of Salem Port. He had not heard such sounds in weeks. But what brought them here, now? Shedding his soggy coat, he ascends to the deck to find it engulfed in sunlight after having been inundated with water. John raises his gaze toward the sky, which is now free of any clouds. The sea is placid, the air warm and refreshing, the breeze light. He brushes off the debris that had accumulated on his clothing and beholds the horizon, where some small, scattered islands have come into view. He blinks in disbelief and opens his eyes again to confirm what he saw. Someone pats his shoulder, humming a tune.

"Those are the islands of the West Indies," the man says. John looks up at the one standing next to him. The captain is telling him that they will harbor here for a day or two while they sell their cargo of lumber and stock up on supplies and tropical fruit. An enchanting calm swathes the deck. Some of the seamen are lying on their backs, sunbathing while their clothes dry. Others are coating wooden surfaces with oil to protect them from the humidity. Some are repairing sails damaged in the storm. Still others, injured in last night's ravages, are having their cuts tended to by the captain's assistant, who is dispensing an extra ration of ale to sip as a temporary anesthetic.

The *Essex* departs a couple of days later, bound for Brazil and a crossing of the equator. John's seasickness has abated, and he's able to sleep a few hours at night without disruption, especially with the more agreeable weather and tranquil sea. From the island, they have procured a small flock of laying hens, and he spends his days feeding the chickens, enjoying the play as he dispenses their corn rations as slowly as possible. When the sun is at midpoint in the sky, the captain calls him to his quarters and offers a lesson on the quadrant and how this instrument is used to determine the ship's location by calculating the angle of the sun above the horizon.

In the evening, he listens raptly to the captain's tall tales about the people of Salem and its seamen. He tells him of the *Grand Turk*, the ship loaded with twenty-eight cannons that was used to seize twenty-five English ships in the heyday of pirating backed by the fledgling American state, making its owner, one Mr. Derby, one of the richest men in the city. In 1784, it sailed under the leadership of Captain Jonathan Ingersoll to the Cape of Good Hope. It was a successful trip, which encouraged its owner to send it on a second trip a year later. It arrived at the Cape eighty-two days after its departure from Salem, but this time it continued its course around the African continent and turned north towards Mauritius, a French colony, to become the first American vessel to anchor there.

Joseph narrates the life of another captain from Salem, Henry Prince, who was accompanied by the famous navigator Nathaniel Bowditch when they worked together on the ship named *Henry* owned by Mr. Derby. Prince later worked in trading and founded the famous West India Goods Store in Salem, before he bought the Derby House near the port, the captain explains.

"Thanks to these two men, we learned much more about our world. If not for the journeys of ships like the *Turk* to the Yemen by way of the Cape of Good Hope, our mission today would be much more difficult than we might expect. We stand today on the shoulders of such great men, to see the world more closely."

John listens to these glorious stories of people from his own town and imagines himself one day as a famous captain helming a ship like the *Turk*. Two weeks after first sighting the Brazilian coast, the Essex turns southeast, allowing the ocean currents and trade winds to carry it lightly towards the western coastline of Africa, like a feather on air, cutting across the middle of the ocean. Land once again disappears from the sailors' sight as they leave South America to penetrate deep into the Atlantic, like a straw hut floating on a vast tank of water whose base is a few miles deep. The captain reviews his map and calculates the upcoming navigation angle, while telling John, "New oceans and lands cannot be discovered unless you have a heart brave enough to allow the shore to disappear from your view."

Those trade winds have played an essential role in conveying sailing ships to new worlds. Adventurers and explorers discovered new sea routes that led them to lands and riches they never imagined.

The appearance of the African coast ahead, stretching south and north as far as the eye can see, stirs mixed feelings in Leon, who tells John about how he was seized from his village somewhere on that shore as a child, brought across this ocean in the stinking, dark hull of a ship not unlike this one, how he shut his eyes to horrors he did not want to remember, and then was sold into slavery.

It does not occur to John, who has never heard a story like this, to ask whether he is a free man now. Leon knows nothing about his mother, father, or siblings. He says he hardly remembers his mother's face, only how she screamed for help when they snatched him out of her hands. But somehow he has come to peace with his fate.

"Always remember, John, the joys and pleasures of life are only showered upon you from the outside, but contentment and peace of mind come from within you. Contentment is a choice, not a result; it is the most beautiful thing you can wear and most precious thing you can own. ... Remember that well."

John asks if Leon has ever tried to find his family, but Leon's vague gesture indicates the futility of that quest. John presses on: why did he not try? But his only answer is the stifled pain in Leon's eyes. John cannot comprehend the feelings of one separated forever from his mother and family, and he certainly does not want to try. All he wants now is to arrive safely at his destination and then retrace his path to his parents.

As they near the southern tip of the African continent, storms begin to swell up and roar anew, but John is more prepared this time, and better acclimated to his surroundings. The ship approaches the Cape of Good Hope to wrap around the turbulent end of the Dark Continent, where oceans meet, like a child hugging Mother Earth at the lowest point of the Old World. The *Essex* continues its course eastward into the Indian Ocean, leaving the Cape far behind. Soon the ship turns north, skirting the eastern shoreline of Africa. Once they are past the Tropic of Capricorn, the weather begins to turn warmer. They are now about a third of the distance between the lower end of the African continent and their destination.

Miles to the east, the island of Madagascar comes into view. It is so large that its end can hardly be seen. At times the *Essex* draws near to those lands, where John spies the wrecks of abandoned ships. The captain reads the questions in the young boy's eyes and tells him tales of how these lands were home to a mob of pirates a century or so earlier. They had adopted the northern part of the island as their base and built a colony for themselves, from which they would attack ships belonging to the navies of that era. What most amazes John is the story of the English sailor Robert Drury, whose ship was wrecked there when he was only seventeen. He became trapped and compelled to serve the island kings as a slave, moving from place to place on the island for fifteen years before he was able to return to England and relate his story.

LOST SON OF SALEM: AN AMERICAN BOY'S ODYSSEY IN THE ARAB WORLD

It is now mid-February 1806, and the *Essex* is approaching the island of Socotra off the tip of the Horn of Africa. Screaming seabirds circle the ship like a chorus, welcoming the strangers. The captain decides to stop for a while to view the exotic rarities on this island that he has heard about from other sailors; he orders the mainsails lowered to let the ship glide more slowly without anchoring, in a bay on the western side of the island.

John listens as the sailors point to the shore and talk of the plants that grow here, many of which are not to be seen anywhere else on the earth. The strangest is the dragon's blood tree, which appears like a huge umbrella stuck firmly in the ground, its domed canopy spreading outwards to protect it from the heat of the sun. It gets its name, he is told, from its blood-red colored sap. The ship continues around several bays and points until some oddly shaped caves appear against the mountain. The *Essex* completes its tour and the sailors unfurl the mainsails again, this time to head west toward Aden, the gateway to the Arabian Peninsula from the Arabian Sea.

Three and a half months and more than twelve thousand miles after its departure from Salem, the *Essex* anchors at the port of Aden. It is time for the ship and all who have sailed in her to rest. Captain Orne disembarks, setting his feet down on the land of Arabia for the first time in his life. Two assistants accompany him, one of whom visited Morocco as a youth and still knows a few words of Arabic. Young John tries to join them, but Joseph Orne, unwilling to risk losing him in this strange land, orders him to stay aboard. His promise to John's father to return him safely echoes in his ears, making him gasp each time he sees the boy step off the ship. He cannot, does not, want to even imagine returning to Salem without him.

The port lies at the foot of a silent volcano connected to the mainland by a narrow strip of land, making the town a peninsula. Thanks to its pivotal location between India and Egypt, it has been subjected to invasions since ancient times. It is said that the city goes back to the beginning of human history, and its name comes from Aden bin Adnan, one of the fathers of the Arabs. But no one can say for certain the age of this ancient city, whose name, Eden in English, is mentioned in a number of holy books. At the time the *Essex* is anchored in its port, it is ruled by the Sultan of Lahej, Al-Abdali.

Captain Joseph and his companions leave the lighthouse behind and find their way through city lanes towards Khormaksar, where some merchants have opened their doors in the early morning. The clothing and faces of the sailors fail to attract a curious glance. This coastal city has known visitors and adventurers for centuries, although few came from the New World, from America. In addition to mosques, which he is seeing for the first time, the captain notices churches and temples, a reflection of the city's openness to cultures from East and West throughout its ancient history. His own country's new constitution comes to his mind—how it guarantees freedom of belief for its citizens, allowing people to choose the religion they wish.

The captain has little difficulty finding someone who can speak English well enough to direct him to the home of Dr. Pringle, the official resident, whom he considers the man most likely able to answer his questions. Captain Orne knows that the coffee markets lie to the northwest of here, in Mokha, Hudayda, and Luhayya, as his uncle explained. Nevertheless, this ancient city is the main gateway to the Arabian Peninsula, a crossroads for traders entering the Red Sea. He hopes that stopping here will help him gather information that could lead to the names of some worthy merchants and provide hints on finding good quality coffee and best prices, giving him an advantage in negotiations when he arrives at those ports.

In a building overlooking the port, Dr. Pringle sips a cup of hot tea and talks with his British companion, Captain Carter, about the contents of the letter he just received from Bombay, informing him that the King's government does not wish to idly stand by and watch what the French, their traditional rivals, are doing in the Red Sea. The letter informs him that the British government plans to send a military contingent to the island of Kamaran to destroy the colonies the French have built there. Pringle muses over the fate of his agreement with Al-Sharif Hamoud and how the latter had allowed Bin Aqeel to lease the island to the French in spite of his promise to instruct him not to do so. Turning to Carter, Pringle says incredulously, "Can you imagine that we even exchanged gifts to celebrate our agreement?"

There is a knock on the door and a softly spoken request to enter.

"Please come in," Pringle announces, his curiosity raised as he recognizes an American accent. Joseph Orne, in a captain's formal coat adorned with gold buttons, steps into the room, leaving his two assistants outside. In spite of the fatigue apparent on his tanned face after more than three months at sea, his youthful but dignified bearing makes a certain impression on the two British men. After exchanging greetings, Captain Orne apprises Pringle of his objectives on this voyage and carefully explains that he is looking to purchase prime Yemeni coffee to carry back to Salem, Massachusetts, a bustling port in the United States.

Pringle can't help wondering dismissively: *Who are these erstwhile colonials, willing to sail such a distance for a coffee bean?*—momentarily forgetting, as he takes a sip of his own cherished tea, how far his own countrymen have been willing to go to nurture their obsessions. In his capacity as British acting resident in Yemen, he is busy with the affairs of the great powers in competition with his country's government, starting with the French and the Ottomans. As for the United States, that rebellious rump of the Empire doesn't really exist on Pringle's map of the world.

"I am told you might be able to guide me to the best coffee ... where can I go?" Orne asks.

"It doesn't matter ... because anywhere you go, you will always be there!" Pringle answers with a sly smile, keeping his eyes on the letter from his government in Bombay.

"I mean, considering my current situation, where can I go?"

"Your current situation has nothing to do with where you go. It only defines where you start," Pringle answers coolly.

"What about this city ... Aden?" Joseph asks, trying to maintain his composure.

"You won't find coffee here in Aden, but you might find the place where Cain buried his brother Abel, as the local legends say," Pringle replies, his thoughts already busy with something else.

"I did not come here looking for the dead, but to purchase some necessities for the living," the captain replies, irked by the Englishman's arrogance and rude manner.

Despite his skills as an experienced seaman, Captain Joseph Orne finds himself feeling like a naïve boy next to this smug British resident with his long years of experience. Pringle appears ready to dismiss Joseph, but he suddenly gets an idea that puts a twinkle in his eye, with nothing to stop him other than his friend Carter, sitting next to him.

Pringle instantly turns more amiable. Putting aside the papers in his hands, he turns toward his visitor and apologizes for not paying closer attention to him, in the midst of all his busyness. He begins to speak about coffee beans: where they are grown in the mountains; how they grow like rubies on trees. He talks as if he were an expert on these beans and advises Captain Orne to go straight to Luhayya. There, he assures him, he will find the choicest Sanaani beans, and he notes the names of some merchants he will find there. To prove the integrity of his information, he suggests that his colleague, Captain Carter, an expert on navigating the Red Sea, accompany Joseph, especially considering the narrow coral reefs one must pass through before entering Luhayya's port, navigating which is not a task for the uninitiated.

The captain is suspicious of this sudden flip in Pringle's tone, especially the offer of services free of charge, but his doubts quickly vanish when Pringle requests a fee for Carter to accompany them as a guide. What Joseph Orne does not know is that the fee request is a mere cover for his real intentions: to use the *Essex* to get a secret message via Carter to his former ally, Al-Sharif Hamoud. He will inform him of his country's intention to send a campaign to destroy the fortifications the French built on Kamaran.

Pringle, a talented schemer, hopes to stay on good terms with Al-Sharif to possibly benefit from him in the future, though this could conflict with his allegiance to his government. He sees no real harm in this, because his government's decision to mount an assault on Kamaran would not be affected by Al-Sharif's prior knowledge of it.

Captain Orne accepts Pringle's proposal without further scrutiny and sails out of Aden on the *Essex* with two additional passengers, the Englishman Captain Carter and his servant, named Haidar, who speaks passable English and sometimes serves as an interpreter, having previously worked for the British resident in Ethiopia.

The *Essex* sails west toward the strait of Bab Al Mandab, which it will reach in just a day and a night. The ship passes through the strait, which is barely twelve miles wide, and penetrates the Red Sea. Heading due north, it continues by Mokha without stopping.

Joseph remembers that his uncle told him he should buy coffee from this region, but Carter's firm insistence that they hurry on to Luhayya, claiming great profits await him there, prompts him to move on in spite of his assistant's objection. William Orne's orders were quite clear in this regard, that the ship should first stop in Mokha. "It won't hurt to continue sailing north a little. I promise you, Uncle, that we will stop in Mokha on the return trip," Joseph says to himself as they sail by the city. He has no idea that this choice will seal the fate of the ship and its passengers.

Essex maintains its course for two more days before reaching an archipelago and turning east, navigating shallow water interspersed with coral reefs. Here, Carter takes over navigation and guides the captain.

Having reached its northernmost destination on the Red Sea, *Essex* drops anchor in the bay of Luhayya just before sunset. This time, Captain Orne permits John to accompany him as he steps onto the wharf, holding his hand to be sure he won't lose sight of the boy. John's hand fidgets when he sees the shore, remembering his carefree days with Henry on the Derby Wharf. He manages to momentarily break from the captain's grasp and hide himself among a crowd of children, only to find the captain, who had managed to keep sight of the boy, standing in front of him once again, shaking his head. And so the two continue on their way, pausing to listen curiously to the sound of the sunset call to prayer that splits the sky.

A mellow Yemeni voice, crying loudly from atop a minaret, chants from a passionate heart: "Allahu Akbar, Allahu Akbar ... La ilaha illa Allah." *God is great, God is great ... There is no god but God.* The two travelers feel safe in this strange place far from home, even though they don't understand a word the muezzin is saying. The voice echoes against the banks of the port and down the city's old pathways, briefly bringing all movement to a halt.

The two return to the ship just before dark, again reminding John of how he had romped, just a few months before, on Salem's wharves. He longs to hear his mother telling him to wash his hands before dinner when he returns home at sunset, but he has learned to keep such yearnings to himself.

Essex spends the night anchored in the port of Luhayya. None of the American seamen have noticed the absence of Carter, who had wasted no time disembarking the ship as soon as possible and headed straight to Al-Sharif Hamoud's home to deliver Pringle's letter. Immediately upon reading it, Al-Sharif is infuriated that Bin Aqeel had the gall to build fortifications for the French despite the letter he sent warning him not to do so.

At first light, Al-Sharif dispatches a ship bearing soldiers to Kamaran to demolish the battlements and seize the goods Bin Aqeel has stored on the island.

Soon after, news of the destruction of the fortifications reaches Bin Aqeel, who has just arrived back in Aden after sailing his ship *Al-Mihdhar* to Mauritius to inspect his farmland. At first he can't believe the news conveyed to him by his younger brother, Abdulrahman, a resident of Mokha who was present in Aden when the *Essex* anchored there. Abdulrahman, a trader of lumber, happens to live next door to Haidar, interpreter for the English officer Captain Carter. Abdulrahman keeps a watchful eye on Haidar's family, checking on their needs when his neighbor is away working.

That is how Abdulrahman came to learn about the meeting between the American captain and Pringle and how Pringle had sent Haidar's boss, Carter, off to Al-Sharif Hamoud to incite his rancor against his old friend Bin Aqeel. Haidar finishes this explanation by asking Abdulrahman to be so good as to attend to his family in Mokha while he is gone with his chief, who will depart soon on the American ship.

Bin Aqeel decides to verify the news for himself before taking his next step. He leaves Aden for Kamaran, where he verifies that it has all been destroyed. All the effort and money spent over the past few weeks is gone with the wind. The structures he had built and the walls he had erected as a shield for French cannons are flattened to the ground. And who is the cause? That interloper Dr. Pringle, the British resident.

In that moment of outrage where a person loses his mind, Bin Aqeel vows revenge, but from whom? His thoughts jump to the easiest and nearest target: Captain Carter, Pringle's envoy to Al-Sharif Hamoud. If not for him, he reasons, Al-Sharif Hamoud would not have destroyed the buildings he built with his own cash. But Carter came aboard an American ship called the *Essex*. And so it shall be, he vows, that this ship and all its passengers shall be the enemy Bin Aqeel seeks to avenge.

Captain Orne has lingered for three weeks in Luhayya, scouring its markets and bouncing from one coffee merchant to another, without finding enough of what he desires. He has managed to purchase some quantities of coffee, but it does not suffice, and large spaces in the hold remain to be filled with precious beans before he can think about returning home.

The captain, preoccupied with business, eases his restrictions on John's movement and allows the boy more freedom to wander the city streets with Leon, especially now that he is reassured of the local population's simple peacefulness. There isn't much John can do other than his favorite activity of going down to the dock in mid-morning to watch the local Arabs in their simple, traditional dishdashas and turbans, constructing boats. There is so much to tell Henry about his trip when he returns, John thinks, and he looks forward to being the one narrating stories from his own experience instead of listening to his mother's tales woven from her imagination.

In the afternoon, John enjoys swimming around the coral reefs teeming with fish, but what most amazes him is the sight of the hump-backed creatures—camels—grazing near the shoreline. What a strange creature to his eyes. His mother had told stories about camels, but they were always in a desert; he'd never imagined them appearing here, near the sea. One day, with Leon, he approaches a camel being straddled by a boy about his age, and walks alongside him for a bit. The boy, grinning, drops down the end of a rope, which John hangs onto and allows himself to be dragged along the sandy beach, an amusing sight that makes Leon laugh.

John sees the boy again, later, when he brings the camels back from grazing, and the two sit down and talk, each in his own language and not knowing what the other is saying. But the content doesn't matter, really. The language of friendship has no words, but rather leaves an impression on the hearts of friends. John understands that the boy's name is Salim. Other than that, everything becomes "Salim" in his eyes. This is the second Arabic word he learns to pronounce after "Allahu Akbar," the phrase the muezzin repeats every day. He repeats his friend's name—Salim, Salim—in a lively singsong that makes his new friend laugh.

As the sun is setting and after Salim has gone home, John climbs the highest mast to not miss the chance to hear the call to prayer. He ponders his view of the town from above, with its citadels and battlements and Tihami houses painted with gypsum whitewash, all framed by the high mountains in the distance. He swivels his head toward the surrounding sea, circled by low green forests of mangrove, while below him the departing sun's rays glisten on the coral reefs. He wishes he could stuff that view and those sounds into a glass bottle and bring it back to Salem as a gift for his mother.

The next day, Captain Joseph takes John with him to see Al-Sharif Hamoud to negotiate the fee for harboring his ship in the port. On the way, he gets a view of Al-Qafl Fort, about which it is said secret catacombs lie beneath that lead to the shoreline. As the days pass, the captain has begun to feel that Pringle was not honest with him when he suggested going to Luhayya instead of Mokha. His assistant has advised him to ask Carter if he had any connection to the rumors of Al-Sharif's boats carrying soldiers to Kamaran Island, but Captain Orne feels it isn't and should not be his business. He knows the limits of his mission well. He is merely the captain of a trade ship, and the last thing he should do is to become a party to a political battle he has nothing to do with, especially in such a remote region about which he knows little. What does not occur to him is that, no matter how hard he tries not to stain his hands with politics, politics could still get its dirty hands on him.

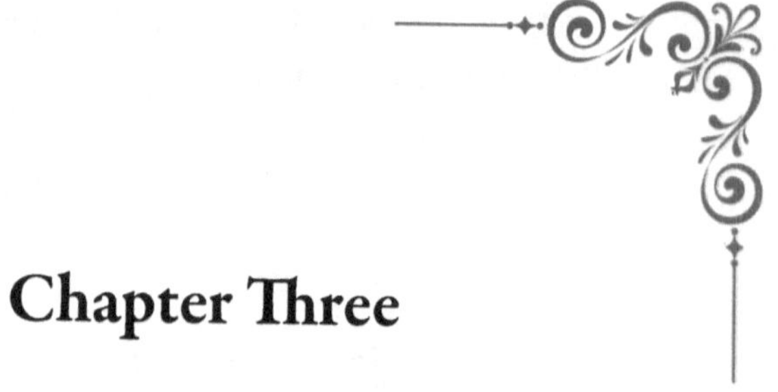

Chapter Three

The *Essex* departs the port of Luhayya and turns southward in the quest for an ample supply of the choice Yemeni coffee beans the markets of Luhayya could not provide. Nearly two months have passed since the ship arrived at the Arabian Peninsula, passing between Aden and Luhayya, now finally turning its bowsprit southward to Hudayda in a final attempt to procure the required stock before heading home. Captain Orne guides the ship slowly through the archipelago surrounding the port of Luhayya, Carter briefly handling the rudder until they have cleared away from the tangled maze of reefs. About two hours later, Kamaran comes into view, a flat plateau formed of coral with mangroves covering large swaths of its northern shores.

Captain Orne decides to stop here to stock up on water, which they did not have the chance to do in Luhayya. Carter, knowing what he does about Bin Aqeel and what happened here, is uncomfortable with this decision and tries to steer Orne away from this idea by suggesting they get their supply of water from Hudayda instead. But the captain, in his ignorance of the situation, insists on stopping here. Carter, afraid to reveal his own deception, says nothing more.

As twilight approaches, the *Essex* anchors off the island's eastern shore, facing some huts constructed by fishermen to use when they come to the island for water. To the west of their mooring place is a grove of fruit trees and the outlet of a small canyon, at whose highest point is an old dam for collecting rain water, which then flows into cisterns for use during dry times. Carter notices another ship moored nearby that appears to be of Indian origin, and it arouses his suspicions. He fears Bin Aqeel may be on the island, and the last thing he wants is a confrontation with him.

The captain launches a small boat and heads to the shore shortly before sunset, along with two of his sailors and Carter. John asks to come along, but Orne, with time passing quickly, directs him to stay aboard. The captain and his small entourage come ashore and ask the locals where they might collect water to cover the ship's needs. A man informs them that they must ask the owner of the island, who has gone into the mosque for sunset prayers and should be leaving shortly with a few servants. Moments later, a plump, relatively short man exiting the mosque stops to wraps a narrow, beaded shawl around his head into a turban, leaving one tail dangling artfully over his chest, and approaches them. His demeanor is that of a wealthy man, of whom the captain had seen few in this part of the world.

Orne approaches the man and introduces himself as well as his companions, before informing him that he is looking for a water source to stock up ahead of their arrival in Hudayda to procure Yemeni coffee. Having learned who the strangers are, the man beams a crafty smile, feigns an overly fervent welcome, and tells them that he is a coffee trader. His coffee, he declares, is better than anything available in Hudayda. He suggests that they stay the night so that he can show and have them taste samples from his stores in the morning.

Captain Orne does not object because, while he has stopped here to collect water, his primary objective is to find coffee to complete his stock. One night on the island couldn't hurt. The man invites them to dinner on his ship, moored not far from the *Essex*, and calls on his servants to prepare his private boat.

All through this exchange, Carter feels a deep apprehension. He turns to one of the soldiers surrounding the man and quietly asks him what his sayyid's name is. His heart nearly drops out of his chest at the answer: it is Bin Aqeel. He wants to pull Orne aside for a few moments to tell him about his role, in conjunction with the British resident, in damaging their host's assets, but the captain is too busy chatting with Bin Aqeel about coffee production as they walk towards his boat. Whereafter, the captain thinks, he and his companions will be treated to a nice dinner of local food by a generous man who will guide him as to where to find the remaining beans to fill his ship's stores.

The boat glides away from the shore, carrying Bin Aqeel to his ship, the *Mihdhar*, with Orne and Carter and a few servants, while the *Essex's* boat sails alongside it, carrying its two sailors. Following these two boats at a distance is another boat full of large, menacing-looking men, who seem unlikely to be ordinary sailors.

Bin Aqeel boards his ship, followed by Orne, then Carter. The British captain keeps trying to whisper in Orne's ear, but every time he is about to finish an unintelligible sentence, Bin Aqeel interrupts by asking Orne about his homeland in Salem, through his personal interpreter. The party sits down at a wooden table on the ship's deck to converse about coffee, the sea, and the still young country, the United States of America.

Also participating in the evening banter is a French officer named Denault, whom Bin Aqeel recruited from Mauritius to survey Kamaran in preparation for building the French settlement. The moon shines brightly as food is served to the guests, at which point Bin Aqeel excuses himself and takes the Frenchman with him to his private quarters.

Carter jumps at the opportunity to urgently murmur in Orne's ear the truth about their host, but alas, he is too late. From the safety of his quarters, Bin Aqeel has instructed a group of his thugs to pounce on the guests. They do not stand a chance of defending themselves against the sudden onslaught of armed men, who proceed to slaughter them in cold blood around the table, wielding dinner knives and daggers that glint in the moonlight and afterward lie in an abandoned heap, spattered with blood.

Taken aback as he emerges from the captain's quarters to view this horrific scene, the Frenchman loudly objects, but Bin Aqeel orders him to be thrust immediately into a cabin below deck.

The thugs then toss the captains' bodies off the ship and chase down and kill the two sailors, equally defenseless, in the small craft that had brought the officers ashore. Bin Aqeel further orders the armed men to proceed in the dark to the *Essex*.

At that moment, John is alone on the deck, enjoying the glittery moonlight reflecting off the water, pondering the calm of night around him and envisioning his town of Salem below this full moon. The other sailors, feeling safe on this warm night with the ship quietly at anchor, have retired to the lower cabins. Suddenly, sharp noises, metallic and vocal, cut through the tranquil air. The noises, John notes, are coming from the ship in the distance, the *Mihdhar*. Minutes later, he spots three boats being launched from the Mihdhar, now headed in the direction of the *Essex*. As they approach, John is able to catch a glimpse of their occupants, which stirs uneasy feelings. He was expecting Captain Joseph with Carter and the two sailors to return, but they are nowhere to be seen. He runs below deck to tell the first mate what he has seen, but he's busy with two other sailors, cleaning the water tank that will be filled if all goes as planned. Preoccupied, the first mate dispatches another sailor to go investigate the matter with John.

The moment the sailor pops his head through the hatch, he receives a deadly blow to his head that sends his limp body tumbling back down the stairs. A firm hand suddenly lands on John's shoulder, yanking him away and dragging him toward a trunk in the galley where he can hide, together with his rescuer. John's ankle twists as he lands in the trunk, but the shock of the moment staves off pain.

The massacre unfolds quickly now. The marauders deftly climb aboard the Essex en masse, easily surprising a crew that was mostly asleep or preparing to go to bed. Slashing swords and daggers make quick work of the American sailors, who are unprepared to grab their own weapons to defend themselves. The attackers throw the corpses overboard, take control of the *Essex,* and rummage through the captain's cabin to plunder whatever money or precious goods they can find, to take back to the Mihdhar.

All the while, poor John and the man hiding with him are listening from inside the galley supplies trunk. They keep their ears cocked as the search continues for anything of value on the ship. Trunks and boxes are opened methodically to loot their contents. As voices come closer, the man hiding with John presses his hand over his small mouth to muffle his rapid panting, fearing it will expose them. John suddenly becomes aware of the pain in his ankle and turns it, knocking over something in the trunk and making a noise that would startle a sleeping person awake. Abruptly, the lid of the trunk rises and hands grab the two to pull them out.

John shivers in fear and cries in the grip of the marauders, while the man hiding with him pleads with their leader to not kill him because he is a Muslim, like them, and not a member of the ship's infidel crew. The man says his name is Haidar—none other than Captain Carter's personal interpreter and escort. The attackers load the booty they've gathered from the *Essex* onto their boats and take it, along with Haidar and little John, to the *Mihdhar.* They will let Bin Aqeel decide the fate of the captives.

At the crack of dawn, they present their booty to their sayyid. They lay out the loot for Bin Aqeel's inspection, and then the one who seems in charge quietly states that there is one more thing they have not presented. The boy feels someone push him forward from behind. Crying and terrified, he tries in vain to remove the shackles from his wrists. Bin Aqeel is astonished to see such a young boy on this ship. Then he turns to Haidar with a questioning look, and Haidar quickly identifies himself, in his most deferential tone, as an innocent resident of Mokha who just happened to be in Luhayya when he noticed the *Essex* preparing to depart and simply asked its captain for transport to his hometown. As for the boy, he says, it seems from the color of his skin, eyes, and hair, and strange language, that he is an American from the same city whence came the American ship crew.

Bin Aqeel, convinced, orders Haidar released and decides, for now, to keep the boy. The head thug, perturbed by this, suggests slaying him would be the wiser course—to remove any threat of having their actions revealed in the future. Bin Aqeel hesitates; he feels dread when he looks upon the innocent face of a child, but the man has a point.

John's trembling blue eyes catch the gaze of Haidar, trying to understand what is happening around him. What are they saying about him? Haidar pities him but cannot say anything in English, lest he reveal his role as Carter's personal translator. Bin Aqeel, reconsidering, casts one last glance at John and orders him to be taken away, hinting at the ultimate resolution of the issue. Once again, a heavy hand drops on the little boy's shoulder and drags him away, bawling and trying to grab anything he can on the vessel's deck, in terror at whatever fate awaits him.

At that tragic moment, a woman wrapped in a long robe suddenly emerges from Bin Aqeel's cabin, screaming and beseeching Bin Aqeel to let the boy live.

"Hasn't enough blood been shed today? How many souls do you need to take to satiate your revenge, O Muhammad, O Bin Aqeel? I beseech you in the name of your grandfather from the land of Mirbat to leave this boy alone! What is this poor child's fault?" If he will but spare him, she says, she will raise the boy as her own son. Bin Aqeel again hesitates in the face of the woman's pleas and the boy's tear-streaked face, while his hired assassin awaits his nod to proceed.

Bin Aqeel recalls the son who died before reaching the age of five, and his heart softens, his blood lust suddenly spent in the wake of all the murder he has ordered this night. He pauses, as if his mind's compass, having gone off-course the day his fury boiled over at what had happened to his island, is now settling back into its normal orientation. He nods to the servant to release the boy and allow his wife, Sayyida Khadija, to take him into the safety of her arms.

The young boy cannot stop crying for several days after the *Essex* catastrophe. No one around him understands his strange language, amplifying his anguish every time he fails to communicate his grief. The Sayyid's wife tries to calm him as best she can, but he wails until his voice is hoarse and refuses to eat. Already slight, he becomes noticeably thinner and weaker. He barely sleeps one or two hours before waking again and returning to his state of muffled wailing and moaning. Those living in the sayyid's household try to conceal this noise whenever Bin Aqeel is about, to avoid disturbing or angering him, afraid of provoking an ominous decision.

Then, abruptly, John stops crying altogether. He no longer has the strength to speak. Sayyida Khadija fears for his life and asks Bin Aqeel to call upon the imam to come and recite some verses from the Qur'an over him, but Bin Aqeel refuses, thinking that it is better to have him mute than talking.

His wife secretly sends a messenger to the imam after 'asr, the late afternoon prayer, calling him to their residence on the island. He obliges and proceeds to recite some verses over the young boy. John shuts his eyes while the imam mumbles words the boy cannot understand. Nevertheless, he feels surprisingly comforted at the sound of it. "... *ir-Rahman ir-Raheem, Maliki yawm id-Deen*"—the Most Gracious, the Most Merciful, Owner of the Day of Judgment—the imam intones. John is finally calmed. He stretches out on his bedding as drowsiness overtakes him and he falls into a deep sleep.

On the other side of the world, as John weeps, his mother Faith prepares supper at home in Salem as she awaits her husband's return. For days now, she has been unable to swallow food. She has had no appetite since John started wailing a week before, though she doesn't know why. Once John stops crying and falls into a deep sleep in Sayyida Khadija's room on Kamaran, a wave of intense weeping overwhelms his mother, as if she is finally crying a backlog of pent-up tears over his departure.

It is as if the volume of tears in the world is constant. If someone stops shedding tears in one place, they will begin to flood another place, such that the volume is equally distributed across the world to maintain the earth's emotions in perfect balance.

As dawn breaks the next day, Sayyida Khadija rejoices at the sight of the boy awakening and pointing to his mouth. She hurries to offer him some dates that she had soaked in fresh water from a nearby well. John starts to devour the dates, but the Sayyid's wife, who knows better, tries to keep him from eating too fast. He has not taken food in a long time.

The boy looks around at his surroundings, realizing his situation has changed. He is no longer on the sayyid's ship, but in his home on Kamaran. Trying to recall what last happened, he remembers the imam's voice reciting words he did not understand. What a strange language, he thinks, resistant to comprehension! It doesn't sound like the Spanish he had heard spoken on the islands they had passed by, heading south from his homeland. And it certainly sounded nothing like the language of the Pawtucket, the native people he had occasionally had contact with in Salem. All he knows of this language is a few words picked up at the ports of Aden and Luhayya: *maa'* (water), *tamr* (dates), *qahwa* (coffee), *bahr* (sea), *sahhab* (clouds), *samaa'* (sky), *Salim.*

"Abdullah, Abdullah." Sayyida Khadija is calling out this name as she pulls him to go outside. The curious eyes of children follow him as she watches over this blond-haired, blue-eyed child. He is like the dolls from distant places that seafarers sometimes bring home for their children to play with. They are captivated by the way he looks and walks, his strange clothing and even stranger speech. One nudges the child next to him, as if he has seen a toy that looks like him, that moves and walks and talks just like this child they are looking at.

"You are Abdullah. Abdullah," she keeps repeating.

He finally realizes that she is calling him by a new name she has chosen for him. "But I'm Paul. John Herman Paul." The children giggle as they hear him speak his last name. It sounds too much like the Arabic word for urine, *bol*. The woman rebukes them and repeats his new name, but he insists on pronouncing his name: "John, John Paul." She refrains from objecting further, lest he become even more insistent and stubborn.

Sayyida Khadija takes him with her as she goes, along with some local fishermen's wives, to fetch water. She removes some of his clothes and, with the help of another woman, lowers him gingerly into a rainwater cistern, to allow him to bathe after many days of lying listlessly in shock. The coolness of the water on an April morning revives the boy, and he peels off the rest of his clothes to immerse himself in the shallow tank. His thin body shivers like a young bird shaking water off its feathers. The Sayyida's eyes follow him, her gaze filled with kindness and compassion, while her neighbor, Zainab, sits down nearby, unable to hide her concern. What, she asks, does the Sayyida intend to do with this boy?

"I will be his mother that did not give birth to him. Allah has sent him to comfort me and compensate Bin Aqeel after his beloved son died in childhood."

"But he is not from us, nor are we like him. Look at the pale color of his skin, like the Christian Englishmen we saw once in Aden. What if his mother appears, asking for him? Do you think his family would leave him here without searching for him?"

"When his family comes looking for him, I will return him to them with gratefulness. But for now, he is my son, until something else comes up."

"I fear that you will become too attached to him, my dear sister. Even if his family comes asking for him, your heart will break at losing him. Would you allow someone to kidnap your beloved child?"

"God forbid! How could you even think such a thing? I am just a caregiver to this child, offering him a home in place of the one he lost, until Allah decrees what must be."

"But ..."

"But what?"

"But you don't even know how to talk with him!"

The day passes quickly while the boy splashes in the water and the ladies gather around the Sayyida to chat. The sight of the blond boy with golden freckles captivates them as he lets out sounds, talking to himself. His eyes follow a flock of migratory birds that have chosen a grove of trees on the island as a rest stop on their way home. Birds, the Sayyida thinks, are but feathers and journeys and songs, created by Allah who gave them trees to rest in, while the humans who admire them put them in cages!

John seems to be singing to them, as if his voice might take flight with the birds toward the home he has left behind on the other side of the world, where his mother might hear him and come to his rescue. The sun rises to the center of the sky, its scorching heat painting the boy's face pink. The Sayyida finally pulls him out of the cistern and encourages him to don the local dress that her servant has brought. John, becoming Abdullah, sheds his American woolen clothing, not realizing that he is shedding nine years of his life, to be clad in Yemeni clothing made of cotton and linen. He tightens an embroidered belt around his waist as he peers at his reflection in the water to behold his new attire. He wishes his mother could be with him to see how he looks in this new adornment—like a young knight that she would describe in her bedtime stories.

As the sun sets on this day, Abdullah sits quietly in front of the Sayyid's house overlooking the sea, contemplating his fate. Will people back home learn of the fate of the ship that left Salem half a year before? If they do learn of it, will his family even know that he was spared from the massacre that wiped out its crew? How much time must pass before they find out? And how much time must pass before they send someone to fetch him? And how much time must pass before they reach him? How much ... how much ...? There are too many questions for the tender young mind of a nine- or ten-year-old to comprehend. How could he? He is a mere child whom the world left behind on an island in the Red Sea near the coast of the Yemen. He has no strategy and no means to return.

A terrifying sight suddenly disturbs his contemplation, and he jumps up in fright. A few hundred yards offshore, the *Essex* groans and tips into the sea, burning to its core at the order of Bin Aqeel, to hide any trace of his actions. The Sayyida instantly pulls him back into the house, covering his eyes out of fear that he might revert to his previous state of uncontrollable sobbing. He rushes to a window to steal a last glimpse of the ship as it is engulfed in flames above the waterline before slipping away into the depths of the sea, taking with it all his memories of the past six months. Abdullah's eyes fill with tears as he watches his only hope vanish. The *Essex* was the lifeline that connected him to his unfathomably distant family, but now it is nothing but a flame extinguished by the waters of the Red Sea. Only a pillar of smoke remains, and soon that too dissipates, along with his hope.

He recalls his mother saying that every life's journey begins with pain, but all will be well in the end. If everything is not well, then it is not yet the end.

Sayyida Khadija rocks Abdullah and sings him lullabies in an attempt to comfort him. She is his only solace in the abyss of grief and loss. But to her, that loss is small compared to the abundant, boundless hopes she has for him. If she had not come out of the cabin when she did on the Sayyid's ship, she reflects, his fate would have been like that of the rest of the Essex's crew. There is much more in store for this boy, her Abdullah.

His life had been like that of his young peers, on a predictable track, until he set foot on that ship that left the port of Salem. If his father had not sent him to join the *Essex*, he would probably have stayed in his hometown, learned a craft, grown up, gotten married, and spent the rest of his life not far from the community where he was born. But those steps aboard the *Essex* set off an astonishing chain of events, still unfolding, that would bring him to an improbable crossing of paths with Bin Aqeel and Sayyida Khadija, an intersection of lives whose meaning was only beginning to be known. And what is life but a myriad of crisscrossing paths?

Bin Aqeel is not the type of man who stays in one place for long. He had barely finished burning the *Essex* before he was ordering his men to pack up and prepare *Mihdhar* to sail the following day. In his own way, he had taken his revenge against those he deemed to have been the cause of demolishing the fortifications he had built on his island for his French customers. He calls his wife in to spend the night with him ... and to consult with her on some matters. He is cognizant of her shrewd opinions and rational mind. He cannot count how many times he has disregarded her advice to his own regret.

For the first time, the Sayyida hears her husband call her *Om* Abdullah, the *mother* of Abdullah, and she likes the sound of it. Om Abdullah prefers not to speak with her husband about events after the fact, but she is never stingy when it comes to voicing her opinion about future plans. She agrees with him that he should change locations now, especially after having failed in his project to present the island as a suitable refuge to the French. She suggests they sail to Muscat, in hopes that Allah will provide for them there.

He asks about the young boy, and she briefly describes his current condition and opines on how he would be the best son for them. She knows that it's too soon to expect him to accept Abdullah as a true member of the family. He is feeling half-hearted relief, tinged with caution. He recognizes now that the manner of taking his revenge was shaped by his anger at the initial culprit, in the person of Dr. Pringle, but didn't actually extend to the man. In fact, his vengeance was so massive and violent that it failed to differentiate between Pringle's envoy and the innocent American sailors coming from the New World, whose ill fate brought them into the middle of a bloody confrontation between him and the Englishmen, though their only part in this conflict had been to allow Carter to board the ship that morning.

As Bin Aqeel's men are busy loading supplies onto *Mihdhar*, someone catches a whiff of a horrible stench. Some corpses have apparently washed up on the island shore. Bin Aqeel, on being informed of this, orders his commander to take up all the bodies so exposed and carry them out to sea far enough so no trace remains, of the *Essex* or of its passengers. Haidar, in proving himself beyond the scope of their revenge, has little choice but to join the Mihdhar sailors in this loathsome task. He comes across one body that makes his stomach lurch: that of Captain Carter, in whose service he has spent many years. He is unmistakable, still clothed in the uniform bearing the British insignia that he was wearing when they left with Captain Orne to meet Bin Aqeel on his ship. His throat has been cut. Haidar notices a silver medallion dangling on a chain around his neck, which he quickly snatches and hides in his pocket before another sailor might notice.

It is the end of April 1806 when the *Mihdhar* raises anchor and sets sail from the eastern shore of Kamaran, headed south bearing Bin Aqeel, his men, a small group of women including his wife, and the young Abdullah.

Abdullah spends his time learning Arabic words and sentences from Haidar, who has agreed with Sayyida Khadija to teach the boy for a small wage. This arrangement avoids any need to spark doubt about his relationship with the English and his service for Carter. After a few days out at sea, *Mihdhar* arrives in the coffee export city of Mokha and anchors offshore at night, although none of the crew members disembark.

Bin Aqeel has noted two British ships anchored in the port, as well as a French one and then a Dutch ship, along with other ships currently loading merchandise. Bin Aqeel hesitates to go to land, especially considering his responsibility for Captain Carter's death. He is well aware that Dr. Pringle resides here in Mokha, and it will be just a matter of time before the news of Carter's disappearance reaches his superiors and they will be gripped with suspicions about Bin Aqeel's involvement. Bin Aqeel asks Haidar to head to the port alone and then to the house of his brother, Abdulrahman Bin Aqeel, and ask him to come meet him.

The city lies tranquil at night, on relatively flat land encircled by a wall interrupted by watch towers. The light of the moon glints off two iron cannons perched atop Tayyar Fort, which protects the town. The town's ancient roads do not faze Haidar, for he knows them well. This is his hometown, after all. He shuffles through the Seashore Gate, one of the city's five gates, and passes through the port plaza, a large open area encircled by chambers built by the Ottomans for their workers levying duties on ships entering the Red Sea. Conical shaped houses are scattered throughout the town. He stops briefly at Al-Shadhili Mosque, with its nine domes, to get his bearings, then continues his route until he arrives at the house of Sayyid Abdulrahman, his neighbor. He knocks on the door and informs him of his brother's request. Mission accomplished, Haidar turns toward his nearby home to find respite after an adventure that nearly took his life.

Abdulrahman hastily leaves his house with a couple of servants, realizing almost immediately that he has forgotten to ask Haidar which gate he used to enter the town. He turns back quickly to catch the man before he disappears, and is told that it was the Seashore Gate. Abdulrahman takes a different route, one headed for the Sandalwood Gate, being careful to avoid raising any suspicion.

A small boat takes Abdulrahman to his brother's ship. *Mihdhar* is not easily missed, anchored as it is only a short distance from the port. He boards the ship to meet with his brother, who is anxious to tell him the latest news verbally, with no middleman. Bin Aqeel learns in turn that Carter's absence is already a matter of concern in the city's tiny British community, though only a short time has passed, and they fear for the life of their envoy.

Bin Aqeel tells his brother everything, including how his revenge struck down the crew of the American ship transporting Carter. Abdulrahman, alarmed by this, reproaches his older brother for his reckless and irresponsible actions and expresses concern for his life, advising him to not stay in Mokha but rather to slip far away from the prying eyes of the English until matters calm down a bit. Abdulrahman, unlike his brother, who has always yearned for influence and power, leans toward peace and quiet. He prefers to remain engrossed in the trade of hardwood and has always left the world of adventure to his brother. The two share a quick dinner before bidding each other goodbye, expressing their hopes to meet again, on land and under better circumstances.

Chapter Four

On the other side of the world, where the Atlantic Ocean meets the land of the northeastern United States of America, in a small wooden house among similar houses in Salem, a thin column of smoke rises from the chimney. In the kitchen, Faith is preparing supper for her husband, who has just returned from his work in the stable. She spreads a frayed linen cloth over the wooden table and the two sit down face to face to share the meal. The mother has not spoken of her son since he departed more than six months prior, although the father has done so, a number of times.

She cannot comprehend the detached way he talks about their son, as if speaking about a neighbor. He rarely mentions him by name, as if trying to distance himself from his emotions, lest his longing come to the surface and expose him. But she hears an underlying tone of guilt in his voice. After all, he is the one who suggested sending their son on a long journey to an unknown land called the Yemen, an Arab land that only a few sailors who knew how to read maps could locate.

Faith feels no relief from the ache of separation from her young one. While her husband distracts himself with his work repairing carriages, her thoughts never leave the boy, not since the moment she stretched her arms out to bid him goodbye while her feet failed to cooperate. She has used whitewash to mark each day since he left on the kitchen wall, until the bag of powder Henry brought for her was all used up and there was no spot left on the walls to mark. She longs for the day when she can stop counting and marking the wall. She wishes to turn the clock back—not to somehow prevent her son from leaving, as this was a fate she cannot change, but rather to plant a farewell kiss on his forehead and hug him in those fleeting moments before time stole him away.

As a mother draws her child towards her in a hug, the topography of her ribcage is revealed, and her scent is exuded as she stamps a kiss on his forehead. He is a part of her that has detached, and she is trying to bring it back home to its original place. Nothing compares to the feelings of a mother deprived of her child, not even how the child feels at being deprived of his mother. A child may be appeased by a substitute mother, even if for a short time while he grows. But the mother will never find a substitute for her child. The burn of longing stays with her as long as she lives.

Life goes on in Salem just as it did the year before, and the year before that, and the year before that. Its port teems with ships bearing merchandise, arriving and departing, returning and sailing away, a vibrant, unwavering movement that never stops to ask who came and who left, who stayed and who travelled. The wharfs are a constant receiving platform for new merchandise. No one notices if someone goes missing other than Faith, who every Sunday leaves church, as other mothers tug their giggling children home, to go stand on a rock overlooking the port, gazing toward the distant horizon, hoping to hear her little boy's laughter mingling with theirs. Perhaps she will see an apparition of her son as the sunlight reflects off the surface of the water, or catch a whiff of his scent wafting on a warm wind from the south, or hear his whisper among the birds migrating north. A shiver runs through her body and she is overcome with dread. More than eight months have passed since John departed.

"Remember me, my son, for I will never forget you. Don't allow anyone to keep you from remembering." *Is he possibly thinking of me now?* she asks her weary self. He never fades from her thoughts except during the few hours while she sleeps. She tries to forget, but how can she? It is the inability to forget rather than the ability to remember that makes us what we are.

Faith returns to sit with her husband at the dinner table, in silence as usual. Silence is an argument impossible to refute. Sometimes it is louder than any scream and more eloquent than any expression.

But one evening, she can't contain the silence any longer. She has not spoken of her son all this time, afraid to open a deep wound that won't heal. Maybe for once she will hear some word of reassurance from her husband.

While her little boy is crying alone on the island of Kamaran, thousands of miles away, she feels a fresh pang creeping into her chest that she cannot explain. She asks her husband to speak to the trader, Mr. Orne, to see if he will send a party out to investigate, to learn why there has been no news from the *Essex*.

"Do you think Mr. Orne did not think of that already? He has more concern than either of us over his ship and wealth and coffee," he says.

"That's not true. He can drink his coffee and he can recover his wealth and his ship could be replaced by another. As for me, my son is irreplaceable. And don't forget that you are the one who persuaded me to let him go in spite of his being so young. Ahh, why did I believe you?!"

Looking at his anguished wife, Herman feels even more guilty. Yes, he was the one who proposed their son's travel.

"Do you know I have not slept one comfortable night since he left? I cannot stop thinking of the day when he will come through this door."

"You talk as if he's only your son ... don't forget that I'm his father, just as you're his mother!" he retorts.

"I know you love him, but, forgive me for saying so, I can't see a trace of your love for him right now. Even in those rare moments when you mention him, you talk about him in such a detached way, as if he's a stranger to us," she replies, her eyes full of reproach.

The father drops his head into tired hands etched into hardened grooves by his carpentry work. The shock of his wife's last words rings in his ears, and he moans aloud. "As if he's a stranger to us," he echoes, "as if he's a stranger to us ... as if he's a stranger to us." He begins to sob, harder then, until it is uncontrollable. It is the mother's turn to be shocked. She has never seen her stoic husband so overwrought. She moves next to him and hugs him to her chest, patting his head. Their tears, freely shed now, cleanse their hearts of months of silence and recrimination. *Love that possesses you and that you do not possess is the one that lasts longer, hurts more, and feels greater.*

They have almost become estranged under the same roof, in two solitudes of grief and loneliness. But now the couple settles into a glimmer of comfort and hope. As Faith retreats to her bed, Herman passes by his son's room upstairs and finds the door open, as it has been since the boy left. For the first time in many months, he peers inside and sees his boy's favorite toy, a ship he made himself with sails taken from an old shirt. It lies on his bed right where he left it ... as if waiting for its counterpart to return.

The *Mihdhar* sets sail at dawn from Mokha, quietly eluding notice, and heads south toward Aden. Since Haidar has left the ship, Abdullah has lost his sole tool for communicating with others and must now depend on himself to learn Arabic well enough to understand what is happening around him. The Qur'an lessons that Sayyida Khadija teaches the boy in the women's quarters help him begin to distinguish sounds and words he could not comprehend well in the beginning. Now he quickly learns to pronounce those difficult letters, like the glottal "ayn" and throaty "kha". *Mokha*, which he been pronouncing as if with a "k"—Makka—now comes closer to the proper sound.

He wanders around the ship, which differs only in small details from those he saw in Salem. He notices a lone passenger, isolated from the rest of the sailors, who has made a stool out of an empty gunpowder barrel, upon which he habitually sits near his cabin door. His white skin and blue military uniform pique the boy's curiosity. He reminds him of some of the soldiers he saw on the islands of the West Indies during his journey on the *Essex*. He certainly could not be African, nor Arab ... could he be from America? If so, this stranger might be his only hope of returning to his family. He approaches with hesitation and apprehension.

"I ... I'm John Paul, but they call me here ... Abdullah," he begins. Before he can finish, the man replies in halting English.

"*Oui*, yes, I know who you are—and where you came from." He quickly continues, anxious to keep his attention.

"I'm Captain Denault, from France. Do you know where France is?" Abdullah shakes his head no. His limited information about the world can hardly help him. He only remembers the name from his father mentioning the French colonies in Louisiana on the Mississippi delta and in Canada, north of Salem.

"I'm not sure where France is, but I think it's about the size of Britain on the other side of the Atlantic Ocean."

"*Oui*, that is correct ... at least for you in America. Come, I have something I want to show you."

The man invites him into his cabin. Abdullah follows reluctantly, looking uneasily around him as he enters the Frenchman's cabin. He notices tools and maps carefully arranged on a worn-out wooden table. They look familiar to him. On closer inspection, he is startled to find these belonged to the *Essex*, and he knows the tools well, especially the surveillance and navigation instruments that Captain Joseph had spent some time describing to him. He winces at the painful memories these objects stir in him and turns, stumbling, to try to escape this shadowy place. For all he knows, Captain Denault could be the one who killed the captain on that dreadful night when he left the *Essex* to answer the invitation to the *Mihdhar*. Denault stops the boy at his cabin door, to calm him. Divining his fears, he swears he had nothing to do with what happened to the crew of the *Essex*. As the boy's panic subsides, Denault grabs a chair and sits down to tell him his story.

Denault worked with the French navy, stationed in the Indian Ocean at their base on the "island of sugar," Mauritius, under the command of General Charles Decaen. The French had seized Mauritius from the Dutch after chasing them out a few decades earlier and declared it a French territory. They set up a naval base to attack the British ships that ventured into nearby waters. Captain Denault received orders from his superiors to go with his colleague, one Captain Chapelain, to the *Mihdhar* to assist Bin Aqeel in the navigation and sailing of a ship he had just brought from Cochin, in India, along with some laborers to build fortifications on the island of Kamaran, having sealed a deal with the Frenchmen to lease the island to them.

When Bin Aqeel discovered what happened to the fortifications his men had built, he unleashed his fury on the American ship that was carrying the British envoy Carter, Denault explained. "And somehow ..."—the captain lowered his eyes in regret—"he ended up taking revenge on the whole crew. Captain Chapelain and I refused to take part in that, which only made Bin Aqeel that much angrier."

After the bloodbath was over, Denault goes on to explain, Bin Aqeel left the command in the hands of his first mate while he sneaked into Captain Chapelain's chamber and cut his throat. Captain Denault was still in shock over all these events when Bin Aqeel's sailors locked him into his cabin, telling him he was to remain a captive in Bin Aqeel's service. Knowing that his relationship of mutual goodwill with his old ally Al-Sharif Hamoud was no longer, and that he had acquired a new enemy in the English, whose influence was expanding in the region, all Bin Aqeel had left to assist him was this Frenchman. So he had decided to spare him.

"I saw what happened to your ship, the *Essex*. Actually, I saw with my own two eyes the murder of Captain Orne and his companions at the hands of Bin Aqeel's men, who locked me up in this cabin. I was, of course, not condoning it, but I had no choice. I am a prisoner here. Come, let me show you something." Captain Denault pulls a small folder from a carefully hidden leather pouch to show it to Abdullah. "This is the *Essex's* record kept by Captain Orne. It bears important information on the trip and all its details. I was able to extract it from the ship's belongings without anyone noticing."

Abdullah takes the record in his hands, touching what is left of the ship that brought him here, the rest now lying on the sea floor. He suddenly raises his head and looks up, his eyes filled with hope.

"Do you have children, Captain Denault?"

"Huh? Yes, two. One of them is a little older than you, but the other I have not seen since he was born." Denault ponders the horizon visible from his cabin's small window. "Coming winter, I will be gone for two years from them and my homeland, but—"

"Could you take me to my family in America? My father would pay you for the trip."

"Oh, sorry, so sorry, I cannot do that. Even if I wanted to, my freedom is restricted and I cannot move around as I wish."

"My mother must be very worried by now about my delay," Abdullah mumbles to himself in misery.

A few days after departing Mokha, in the first week of May 1806, *Mihdhar* reaches Aden, one of the most important ports of the Old World. It anchors at its ancient harbor below Sirah Fortress, which rises imposingly atop an island separated from the mainland by a narrow waterway of one hundred yards. Abdullah recalls the city well, having arrived there just a few weeks before on the *Essex*, still under the full care of its crew and watchful eye of its captain. But the circumstances are quite different now. He is alone in a strange land, with no inkling of what lies in store. The closest people to him, those who held the hope of his safe return to his family, are gone.

Their arrival comes a few short hours before a French ship docks nearby on Sirah Island, as if it had a prior appointment.

Bin Aqeel sends a scout before sunset to survey the ships in the port. He is worried about the British and fears they may chase him. He also takes advantage of Captain Denault's presence to inquire about the ship that is raising the French flag. Denault spies it through his telescope and observes the workers on board from a distance.

"That is *Le Vigilant*, no doubt about it. Its captain is Captain Guilliers, as I recall. I once worked with him while sailing in the Red Sea to Jiddah."

"Are you sure of what you say?" asks Bin Aqeel.

"As sure as I stand before you."

"Do you know anything about the nature of this captain and his mission?"

"I remember that he was ill-natured—" Denault replies.

"All Frenchmen I have met are like that," Bin Aqeel interjects impatiently. "But what brings him here?"

Bin Aqeel is aware that some military ships engage in piracy, despite flying the flag of their homeland, to cover some expenses their governments fail to pay for, and sometimes to satisfy the personal desires of their commanders. Perhaps, he thinks, Captain Guilliers is a pirate in French officer's clothing. Bin Aqeel prefers to deal with a pirate rather than a government officer. In fact, he thinks a pirate's promise is more reliable than that of a government official, whose orders could change from one moment to the next.

The following morning, Bin Aqeel offers his services to the French Captain Guilliers to supply his ship with water and fuel. He also orders his men to prepare a meal for the French ship's crew, then goes to meet him in the afternoon. Bin Aqeel discovers in this meeting that the captain is aware of the agreement between Bin Aqeel and his country's government regarding use of Kamaran. He jumps at the opportunity to ask Captain Guilliers to deliver a letter to General Decaen, the ruler of Mauritius, explaining how he was stymied by Al-Sharif Hamoud following the Englishmen's machinations. He reiterates his desire to cooperate with them and his commitment to their agreement.

Bin Aqeel is keenly aware that the British are expanding their influence and that his relationship with them, even before the latest unpleasantness, has been strained. Therefore, he tells the captain, he wishes to maintain ties of goodwill with the French and not lose them, too, despite their waning role in the Red Sea since the Ottoman-British alliance pushed Napoleon out of Egypt.

Bin Aqeel returns to his ship to share tea with his wife in his private cabin. She is his cousin, descending from the Sharif family, and he always entertains her opinions even though she often regards his actions as either reckless or hasty. He asks her about settling in Aden and visiting its ruler, the sultan of Lahj, but she maintains her previous opinion that they should head for Muscat or settle in their hometown of Mirbat, where they grew up and their families reside. She is thinking of young Abdullah and advocates for taking a break from this life of wandering, somewhere far from the enemies chasing her husband.

Bin Aqeel passes the night without disclosing his decision to his wife. He rises early and heads north into the interior of Yemen with a few of his men, on camelback. They pass through ancient Sabr, a long range of hills covered with patches of broken ancient clay pots, so many that the soil has turned red from their crumbling remains. The hills take them to Lahj, a land of palaces made of marble columns and adobe bricks.

Bin Aqeel is anticipating presenting to the Sultan the gifts he has brought with him, but is surprised to find himself rebuffed. The Sultan refuses to receive him, saying that he is not welcome in the sultanate. He turns his entourage around and decides to depart Aden immediately, after nearly ten days there.

The Sultan of Lahj's scouts, he realizes, must have informed him that Bin Aqeel was suspected of being embroiled in some action that has incited British hostility. The Sultan does not wish to house an enemy of the British, considering their growing influence. So the *Mihdhar* turns its back to the African coast and sails towards Muscat on the eastern edge of the Arabian Peninsula, another journey in its long list of journeys.

A few days following the decimation of the *Essex's* crew, bodies are again washing up on shore: at least seven are found south of Kamaran, carried on currents flowing toward Hudaydah, and two others near Luhayya, north of Kamaran. Local fishermen spread the news that these strange corpses are white-skinned people. At first, the residents surmise a boat has sunk and the crew drowned in the deep sea, not an unusual occurrence. But a closer look suggests these men were murdered, not drowned. The news travels fast to Dr. Pringle in Mokha, who is awaiting the arrival of a Mr. Harris, a British army captain stationed at Bombay. At the time, Mr. Harris is not far from one of the sites near Hudaydah where some of the corpses appeared. Curious about the rumor he has heard, he asks to stop and venture out on a small boat to investigate the story.

At a site northwest of Hudaydah near Al-Araj, between the estuaries of the Sirdad and Siham Valleys, Mr. Harris wades onto the sandy shore with some sailors and a local guide who has promised to take them to the site where two bodies were found. The guide dashes ahead to shoo away birds gathering around the corpses. One appears to be a young man in his twenties. Although Harris cannot determine his identity, his clothing suggests he was a member of an American vessel's crew. As for the other corpse, he suspects it is one Captain Carter, or what is left of the poor man. Harris has met Carter previously, and though a precise identification is difficult from the bloated body, the dress uniform he is wearing—a blue double-breasted coat adorned with two columns of brass buttons—removes all doubt that this was a British naval officer. Mr. Harris returns to his ship after ordering his sailors to bury the bodies respectfully in soil not far from the shore, and to place markers over their graves, each with an inscription: *Here lies an unidentified American man in the prime of his life who met his fate in Yemen. From the dust he came, and to dust he returns.*

Harris sails on to Mokha, where Pringle is waiting for him. The two confer over the information each has gathered and a picture of the crime begins to come into focus. Pringle is certain the American sailor was part of the crew of the *Essex*, the ship on which his emissary had sailed a few weeks before and which has not been seen since sailing from Luhayya. It seems Bin Aqeel's actions have put him further beyond the pale than he was in merely seeking to lease the use of Kamaran to the French. His hands are now stained with blood, and even worse for Bin Aqeel is that one of his victims was a British captain.

"But the question remains, what motive would lead a man like Bin Aqeel, who is mostly concerned with trade and making money, to commit such a maniacal act as this?" Pringle wonders.

"Do you doubt that he is responsible for these events?" Harris says.

"No, I have no doubt about that, but you know very well that I must find a direct link between Bin Aqeel and the fate of the *Essex* in the report I submit to Bombay."

"Very well, then you will need to extract testimony from one of Bin Aqeel's men as to what happened."

"I doubt that's possible. I have it on good authority that those who work with him are fiercely loyal to their master, or at least deeply fear his anger."

"In that case, your best hope is to find a survivor, someone who was not siding with Bin Aqeel on this."

"You mean from the *Essex's* crew?"

"Or the *Mihdhar*. Don't forget that Carter was not actually one of the crew of the betrayed ship, the *Essex*, though he was sailing on it."

"But ..."

"But what?"

"But what I don't understand is, what made Carter board an American ship? What was his mission in the first place?"

Pringle stammers a bit before replying, as if searching for an answer. "Perhaps ... perhaps he was looking for someone to deliver him."

"Deliver him? Deliver him where ... and why?"

Pringle stops short of offering any answers, telling himself to leave the matter as is and not give it too much weight. Otherwise, he might create a problem that was not there in the first place.

Harris stays for a few days in Mokha and is able to meet with the captain of an American ship that happens to be there, preparing to return home after procuring its cargo of coffee. Harris informs Captain Gardner of what he thinks happened to the *Essex* so that he may deliver the sad news to its owners, especially the waiting relatives of its crew.

"If a person spends his life waiting for the coming storm, he'll never enjoy a sunny day." This is how Harris closes his conversation with the American captain. Captain Gardner needs no more substantiation than that brought forward by a British officer. His prior suspicions, based on rumors he'd heard on a several-day stop in Luhayya, are now confirmed. He is convinced of what Harris relates to him and assumes there are no survivors.

Pringle wastes no time before seeking out answers to his own questions. The scouts he has sent out to search for any information in the back alleys of Mokha overheard someone boasting loudly of his supposed heroism on the American ship destroyed by Bin Aqeel. The voice was none other than that of Haidar, whom Bin Aqeel had released from the ship. Once Haidar realizes that eyes are watching him and tracking his movements, he decides to flee northward in the direction of the town of Bayt al-Faqih, leaving his family and hometown until things quiet down.

But he has barely left Mokha when he is intercepted by men sent by the local ruler, who threaten him with death if he speaks with the English about Bin Aqeel. Pringle's spies subsequently catch up with Haidar and bring him back to Mokha so Pringle can question him. At first, he refuses to talk, fearing the wrath of the local ruler's men, though he knows Pringle personally from when he was Carter's chaperone. Only after Pringle secures his safety—by informing the local ruler that Haidar is now under the protection of the British government, thus convincing him to keep his distance—does he reveal what he experienced at Bin Aqeel's hands.

Haidar's testimony as to what transpired on the *Essex* is definitive proof of Bin Aqeel's involvement in Captain Carter's death, burning the American ship, and looting its contents. The silver medallion Haidar pulled from Carter's pocket when he was compelled to help Bin Aqeel's sailors move the bodies offers further cold, hard evidence. Pringle prepares a detailed report and sends it urgently to the British government seat in Bombay, paving the way for Bin Aqeel to become its primary wanted suspect in those seas.

Released after providing all of this information, Haidar is preparing to leave when Harris takes a seat near Pringle in his small office. In his palm, Pringle holds Carter's medallion; contemplating it stirs up memories. He turns to his companion and says, nodding toward Haidar: "That's the man I told you about. He's the sole survivor of the *Essex's* passengers."

Haidar, hearing this last comment, adds on his way out: "Don't forget little John."

Pringle, startled, rushes to catch him before he leaves. "What? I thought you said there were no survivors!"

"I didn't say that," Haidar replies coolly.

"Why didn't you tell me?" Pringle says, infuriated.

"You didn't ask. All you cared about was Bin Aqeel and how he burned down the American ship."

"Fine, then. So, who is this John?" Pringle asks, tamping down his anger at this shifty little man.

"All I know is that he was one of the travelers on the vessel. A young American child whose life Bin Aqeel decided to spare, as he did mine. Poor thing, how will he live alone here?"

Haidar's words make Harris recall a conversation he had with the American Captain Gardner a few days before, as he was relaying the official statement of the *Essex's* fate and the murder of all of its passengers. He turns to Pringle to ask when he last saw Captain Gardner.

"Two days ago," he replies, and with that, Harris rushes out, making his way to the port in hopes of finding Captain Gardner so he can tell him of the lone survivor. At the dock, there is no sign of Gardner's ship. He rushes to the customs building to search the ship registry and discovers Gardner departed the night before to return to his homeland. His heart sinks as he remembers the American's parting words, about waiting for the storm. *This will be a false storm for a family over there.*

In Bombay, on the western coast of India, the jewel of the British Crown's colonies, several vessels of the Royal Navy fleet lie at anchor. One is the ship commanded by Captain Seton, the British resident in Muscat, who has just returned from a campaign he led against the Qasimi tribe. He is responding to new orders from his superiors to send a message to Al-Sharif Hamoud, the ruler of Abu Arish, warning him not to sell Kamaran to Bin Aqeel. This was the ship whose mission had prompted Pringle to send his envoy Carter to deliver a secret message to Al-Sharif Hamoud, warning him of his government's potential invasion of Kamaran if he did not withdraw from his deal with Bin Aqeel.

Pringle's last report to Bombay has resulted in a change to Seton's instructions. He is now ordered to arrest Bin Aqeel and destroy any fortifications he might find on Kamaran. Having requested additional reinforcements, Seton was supplied with two battleships and two frigates from the Royal Navy's fleet. In effect, the British navy is about to wage war against Bin Aqeel.

The military vessels reach Kamaran by the end of summer to discover that the fortifications Bin Aqeel had built under the supervision of the French have already been completely removed, so the fleet of five ships turns around and heads towards Luhayya, anchoring there to allow Seton to meet with Al-Sharif Hamoud and inform him of his orders to arrest Bin Aqeel and deliver him to the government seat in Bombay.

Al-Sharif Hamoud explains that he is the one who ordered the demolition of the fortifications, but he does not mention the secret letter he received from Pringle through Carter telling him of the British government's intention to invade the island if the fortifications remained. He still doesn't know whether Pringle's superiors were aware of the role Pringle had played in warning him, so he keeps his relationship with their administrator in Mokha confidential. It's possible, he thinks, that Pringle acted on his own accord, which bodes well for the possibility of benefiting from communication with the British resident outside the government framework.

Al-Sharif does not lack for wisdom and political savvy, which has helped him maintain the rule of discord and continue communicating with enemies and friends equally. Al-Sharif claims he destroyed the fortifications based on instructions from Ibn Saud, who also requested he deliver Bin Aqeel to Al-Diriyah in shackles.

It is June 1806, and somewhere in the Arabian Sea, many miles southeast of Mukalla, the *Mihdhar* unfurls its sails to take advantage of the seasonal southern winds, which push the ship northeastward at top speed, towards the prosperous city of Muscat, where Al-Sayyid Saeed bin Sultan resides. Aboard are Bin Aqeel, his wife, his sailors, servants, slaves, and some children and women, as well as the French Captain Denault and little American Abdullah. Bin Aqeel's vigilant eye, paired with Denault's navigation skills, and their shared alertness to any vessel flying the British flag, enable the *Mihdhar* to stay out of sight of Captain Seton and the fleet out of Bombay charged with arresting him.

With the humid summer breezes, life onboard goes on as usual. None of the *Mihdhar's* passengers senses danger, though hostile vessels speed along parallel to the *Mihdhar's* route and there's always a chance, however minute, of confluence and confrontation, at which point the predetermined result will be in favor of the British.

Sayyida Khadija persists in teaching religion and Arabic language to the children of sailors working with her husband out at sea, with a special focus on Abdullah. She dedicates more time to him than the other children, in spite of the misgivings of her female companions—especially Zainab, who has not ceased discouraging her resolve to nurture the boy. As Zainab sees it, his sole inclination will be to return to his family if he gets the chance.

Despite the bond of friendship between the two women, who grew up together as neighbors, Zainab envies Sayyida Khadija, the lady of influence and lineage and the wife of Al-Sayyid. As for Sayyida Khadija, she knows full well that if this boy's fate is to live in this part of the world, to have a promising future he must be able to coexist with the people of the land. And the key to that is to master their language, then learn their culture and religion.

As the *Mihdhar* draws near the coast of Dhofar, Sayyida Khadija calls to Abdullah and takes him by the hand, pointing to Mirbat as they sail by. This is the village where her husband grew up, just east of Salalah. She speaks to him in simple, unpretentious Arabic about her husband and his family of upright lineage, descendants of the Prophet Muhammad, the "Ashraf"—honorable ones—who are given the title of Sayyid, specifically the house of Al-Saqqaf, of the kinfolk of Aal Ba-Alawi. She describes how their lineage reaches back all the way to the daughter of their religion's Prophet. Long ago, their ancestors travelled to Hadhramawt, and some of them settled in the Dhofar region, in the towns of Mirbat, Salalah, and Taqah, and some nearby villages. Their grandfather was Muhammad bin Ali, famously known as the founder of Mirbat.

Abdullah listens avidly as the Sayyida recounts how the people of Hadhramawt toured the earth and traveled across the seas to reach the Far East, a story that reminds him of his mother's bedtime tales of the waves of emigration from Europe to his homeland in America, and about the Native Americans that would bring their goods to sell in Salem's markets. Abdullah asks, in his clumsy Arabic, whether they will stop in Mirbat, but the Sayyida informs him that they are headed instead for Muscat. They cannot risk stopping in Mirbat, much as her husband might wish to visit his hometown. She, of course, was the one who advised her husband to go to Muscat after his project on Kamaran foundered, his relationship with his old ally crumbled, and the Sultan of Lahj deserted him.

Sayyida Khadija is dubious about the wisdom of her husband's actions, which led directly to Bin Aqeel's current troubles, and her attempt at justifying his behavior is therefore unconvincing.

Bin Aqeel had worked for months to seal a deal with the French to lease the island to them, after paying Al-Sharif Hamoud for it in full, she explains, and then searched for builders and fetched equipment from Mauritius—only to return and find that all of his pain and effort had been in vain, due to the scheming Englishman's plan to wedge enmity between himself and his old ally and friend. And that's why he ordered the *Essex* burned; it had been carrying that British captain.

Sayyida Khadija rattles on, as much to amuse herself as to explain things to the boy. She says she feels it's time for him to know who they are and to understand their familial heritage, contrary to whatever misrepresentations he may hear from others, or what differing interpretations may be presented to him by some person horrified by recent events. They are not murderers or kidnappers of children or bloodthirsty pirates, as their English enemies imagine them to be, or even as some of their own flesh and blood perceive them. They are like any other family, searching for ways to make a living, aspiring to a better future for their offspring.

Abdullah doesn't understand all of what the Sayyida is saying; in fact, he's not sure she's really talking for his benefit. Nor is he ready to accept any excuses or justification for what happened to him. He still feels anguish at losing the whole crew of the ship that brought him here. After his own family, he felt closest to them. He feels he is the victim of kidnapping in this strange land and hopes it's just a matter of time before he returns to his family—especially his mother. He has no doubt that, somewhere on the other side of the earth, she is waiting for him.

On a sizzling hot day, the *Mihdhar* arrives at Muscat. The ship slows after the crew furls the mainsails and anchors in the port's channel, where the Al-Jalali Fort stands atop a rocky outcrop overlooking the Gulf of Oman. Paired with its companion, Fort Al-Mirani, the two fortresses stand as loyal guards of the city, protecting it from greedy invaders. The channel is no more than ten fathoms deep; crystal-clear waters where one may easily view the sea floor.

At present, the city is ruled by Al-Sayyid Saeed bin Sultan, of the House of Busaid, whose original founder died a mere three decades before. Bin Aqeel hops off the ship and rushes across the dock with one of his assistants, hurrying to avoid being noticed by anyone. He does not know the extent of the Englishmen's contact with the ruler of Muscat, but he knows the city's network of roads well, having visited many times in the past. He has maintained mutual geniality with some of the city's influential figures, bonded by longstanding business relations. The city appears the same as the last time he saw it, teeming with movement among the local Omanis, including Arabs and Belushis, and a mix of Persians, Indians, Africans, and a few pale-skinned Europeans, all there for commercial interests.

Bin Aqeel has no trouble locating a place to rent, finding a clean and spacious house not far from the port that he deems appropriate to house his family and helpers. There is an adjacent plot of land, which he also leases and pays for immediately and then orders some of his workers to build a wall around it to protect it from view. With this done, Bin Aqeel's men begin to unload the *Mihdhar's* cargo and store the goods brought from Yemen in the leased house. As for their acquisitions from the *Essex*, the men wait until sundown to unload these items, storing them under the protection of darkness in the adjacent lot.

Just two days after the Mihdhar anchored, Bin Aqeel and his men have completed the move onto land, leaving a small crew on the ship to guard it.

"Abdullah, let us go," Sayyida Khadija calls cheerfully as they disembark. It has been nearly five months since Abdullah arrived in the land of the Arabs. He is becoming accustomed to his new name, his ear more familiar with it when called. As they walk, he holds her hand, or rather Sayyida Khadija holds his; she is loath to let go of him for even a moment as she leads him to their new home in Muscat. She tells him this city is where they will be staying, God willing. This is the first time the boy has set his feet in Oman, here at the most northern point of the country, on the Gulf of Oman.

The boy, Sayyida Khadija, and one of her servants pass through the narrow city streets, past a market swarming with people, where the Sayyida stops to purchase a few items. Abdullah clings to her out of fear of getting lost. He knows no one here besides her. The various goods on display in Muscat remind him of the traders of Salem and its famous port boardwalk, where he used to play with his friend Henry. Abdullah's eyes follow slow-moving specks of light playing over the wicker baskets filled with dates. Gazing overhead, he sees their origin is in the weather-worn woven straw covering that shields shoppers from the blazing rays of sun.

The Sayyida tugs him along as they continue on, past the slave market where men and women are being displayed as merchandise waiting for buyers. He listens to the slave trader as he points to the bodies of some weary women, bringing out one after another to climb a raised stage so buyers can make their bids. The price of a woman is almost double that of a man. One of them casts her eyes towards him, giving him a look he will never forget as he notices the shackle on her ankle pressing into her veins. Sweat pours down her haggard body as she drags the iron chain locked on her foot that connects her with a companion who is in similar distress. He could turn his eyes away, but he knows this scene will never disappear from his mind. As soon as one woman is sold, the slave trader hastily leans over to remove the lock from her ankle and turn her over to her new master. One cannot expect to subjugate another by shackling their feet without having to stoop low to do so!

The days pass swiftly for Bin Aqeel as he occupies himself with selling the goods—coffee and lumber—that he brought with him from Yemen, at a handsome profit. He is also able to sell a large portion of the items he looted from the Essex and pass on some to local tradesmen whom he trusts to sell them for him. The relative safety of Muscat and distance from the disastrous events he was involved in prompt him to open a shop near the port where he can pursue his buying and selling activities with great enthusiasm.

Every evening, he proudly relates the news of his daily successes to his wife. He gives her credit for advising him to come here, but Sayyida Khadija is engrossed in caring for her boy, who has come down with fever and hasn't been out of bed for days. Abdullah, she reasons, can't tolerate such oppressive heat, having come from the cold land of North America, which she has heard is covered with snow and ice. For this reason, the Sayyida asks permission from her husband to take the boy to the nearby mountains, in hopes he will be more comfortable there. Perhaps the new place is simply more than he can tolerate.

Feeling buoyed by his new role as one of the most influential traders in the city and calmed by a sense of security and impregnability in Muscat, Bin Aqeel decides to request a meeting with its new young ruler, Al-Sayyid Saeed. He does not have to wait long before receiving an acceptance letter delivered by the sultan's delegate, who personally escorts him to the ruler's residence. Bin Aqeel hopes to receive the acceptance and blessings of Al-Sayyid Saeed bin Sultan, that he might protect him and consider him as one of his countrymen. And this is the actual result of the brief visit.

The ruler receives him, contrary to custom, in his private office rather than the assembly hall for greeting guests. This indicates a perception that the meeting is related to business rather than for becoming acquainted and exchanging cordialities. Bin Aqeel shuffles into a square room within the palace, its high white walls punctuated by vertical, narrowly rectangular openings that allow light to enter the room. Colored wood shelves are lined with decorative items such as crystals, daggers, and hanging swords. A simple Persian rug covers the floor, and a few wooden chairs covered with silk cushions are scattered about. At the end of the room is a table bearing some papers and writing items. Behind it stands a tall, slim young man: Al-Sayyid Saeed bin Sultan.

Bin Aqeel is astonished at the simplicity of the room and even more amazed at the humbleness of Al-Sayyid Saeed. He is impressed, in spite of the man's youth, with his manner of speech, as he starts out confidently and calmly explaining his thoughts on free trade with no discrimination and of his aspiration to build a mercantile marine fleet supported by the Omani naval forces, which would solidify relations with China, India, Ceylon, Iran, and East Africa.

Bin Aqeel departs the Sultan's residence after arranging an appointment for the Sultan to honor him with a visit to his ship, the *Mihdhar*. This all is much more than he could have hoped for from this brief visit. Bin Aqeel returns to his store impressed with the youthful Sultan's personality, musing within himself that if this young man is predestined to have a full life, then Oman will certainly have a bright future under his rule, and he will have a memorable role in his country's history and development.

Just a few days later, Sultan Saeed is onboard the *Mihdhar* in response to Bin Aqeel's invitation, touring the ship and inspecting its masts and sails. Bin Aqeel explains how he brought and sailed it from Mauritius, where it had been named the *Dove of Bombay*, before he changed its name to Al-Mihdhar. The youthful Sultan does not hide his admiration of the ship, so Bin Aqeel jumps at the opportunity to offer it to him as a gift—and to cement the friendship he has been hoping for. The Sultan kindly refuses but insists instead on purchasing the ship, asking Bin Aqeel to set the price he desires.

Bin Aqeel continues to visit the ruler's diwan, which is usually reserved for officially invited delegations and commercial interest partners. But sometimes the Sultan calls him in personally to seek his advice regarding the port and ship docks or commercial matters and interests.

Bin Aqeel's friendly relationship with the Sultan kindles the rancor of some of his competitors, who see him as a threat to their interests. Some who are aware of his past send news to the British governor in Bombay to inform them that Bin Aqeel is in Muscat and not in Kamaran or southern Yemen, as they had thought. Among these competitors is the trade representative of Al-Sayyid Saeed bin Sultan; he hints to the Sultan that Bin Aqeel's choice to settle in Muscat might be motivated by political goals and that he desires to seek local government positions, not for the purely commercial incentive, as he claims. But the vigilant Sultan demands proof of this before responding to what may only be gossip. He assumes that Bin Aqeel's reason for staying in his country is just as he described it to everyone—that is, he longs for free trade—until otherwise proven.

Sayyida Khadija returns to Muscat after spending a few weeks in the nearby mountains with Abdullah, who has recovered from the fever, to find that her husband has sold his ship and dismissed its sailors, maintaining just a few slaves in his home and some assistants in his store. Most of the workers that had accompanied him, as well as the ship's crew, have gone their separate ways.

Even Captain Denault has found a ship headed for Mauritius and agreed with its owner to sail it as captain, in return for the travel. But before he leaves, he quietly hands over to Abdullah the travel log of the *Essex* that he had secretly recovered from Captain Orne's belongings. Denault sees the boy as the true heir of that ship. He hands him the small book, pressing it between his hands as if delivering a trust, asking him to keep it safe until he grows older. Abdullah does not know the true value of this book, but Denault's eyes impress on him that this is a weighty matter and that he must deliver these carefully bound pages to the *Essex's* owner when he grows up and finds a way to return.

The significance of the record, as Denault knows, lies in the details it contains of the trip from the moment it departed the port of Salem until a few short hours before its destined fate. It is like a diary that documents all the events that transpired on the ship and on the lands it visited, indicating the days and hours.

But its true value might be found in the pages that Abdullah would add in the days ahead, completing the story of his life.

On a warm winter morning in Muscat, one of Bin Aqeel's assistants stands on the wharf peering through a telescope, as he does every day, scrutinizing a naval vessel that has caught his attention with its cannons facing the port. Suddenly, he notices the British flag flapping atop the ship's mast. His heart races as he watches the ship approach the dock. The time has come to apprise his boss of what he has anticipated daily. He dashes to the Sayyid's home to awaken him and tell him what he saw.

Bin Aqeel wastes no time, quickly waking the rest of the house to set off a string of actions he has carefully set out. All that remains is to activate his plan. He sends someone to a merchant who handles rapid-cargo ships to lease a ship in a hurry. Then he orders his store assistants to transfer all his merchandise to the ship, and his slaves to move all his household goods quickly to the ship as well. Before nightfall, Bin Aqeel and his family are on board; the anchors are raised and the sails unfurled, and the ship heads south for Mirbat, leaving behind one assistant to pay the outstanding rent and any remaining debts.

The news of Bin Aqeel's sudden disappearance spreads quickly, along with various rumors about why he left. Some say he left to escape debts owed, while others surmised that he had committed a crime, especially because there was a European-looking child living in his house. Perhaps he kidnapped him from his family, the rumor-mongers speculate. But these rumors dissipate as soon as the real reason is revealed, when the head of the British ship, Captain Cramer, meets with Al-Sayyid Saeed bin Sultan and demands he turn Bin Aqeel over to him. The English captain is enraged to learn that Bin Aqeel has escaped and blames Al-Sayyid Saeed for facilitating it. The Sultan rebuts this accusation, hoping to prevent the situation from escalating. The captain's visit is all the more unwelcome after he had the audacity to accuse him of being involved.

The truth is, he has always known Bin Aqeel was wanted by the British authorities, although the man himself had never revealed that to him. Bin Aqeel's situation has allowed the Sultan to rebuff claims by his competitors and the gossipers that he was only out for power and influence. He recognizes that Bin Aqeel's position on Muscat was weaker than that of someone seeking political power; in fact, he was more akin to a refugee seeking the protection of the Sultan.

Chapter Five

About two miles off the port of Salem, Captain Gardner's ship has nearly completed the long journey from Yemen. Although the ship already unloaded half of its cargo in Boston, to the south, a heavy load continues to weigh on the captain, one he must deliver as soon as he arrives. Gardner considers simply sending a letter to the people of Salem, to spare himself the pain of personally delivering news his ship could hardly bear. His assistants object, saying that bad news should be spoken, not written, so that it stops hearts only once, rather than being repeated endlessly in written lines.

The ship lowers its anchor at Derby Wharf, the very wharf from which the *Essex* launched nearly a year before. Captain Gardner disembarks and asks a worker for directions to the office of Mr. Orne, in a building not far from the port. Gardner recalls meeting with Orne two years before in Boston, while they attended a gathering of traders to negotiate customs tariffs. He remembers well how Orne opened his speech, "I have some good news and some bad news for you. As for the good news, there is no need to worry because you cannot change what has already occurred. And as for the bad news, however much you try, you cannot change what has already occurred."

Gardner is not surprised at Orne's stoic reaction to the confirmation of his ship's fate. Orne tells him he has long expected something terrible had befallen the ship after all reports of sightings had ceased.

"At this point, any new news would invariably be bad," he tells him. "This is how I have made peace with it." Gardner asks if he plans to announce the news now or wait until the evening, when people return to their homes. He answers, "Better to do it right now, because bad news, unlike wine, does not improve with age." Orne bids Gardner goodbye and steps out to the local newspaper office to see that the news is announced in the next edition. He then continues on to the homes of the families of those presumed dead. He feels it best to inform them in person before night falls and they learn the fate of their loved ones in print.

On this day, the fifteenth of October 1806, we have received news from the office of Mr. William Orne, the well-known proprietor in our town, who states that his ship called The Essex sank during its journey to Mokha in the Yemen. All of its passengers and crew lost their lives. This newspaper offers its sincere condolences to the families of the victims, Salem's courageous sons.

This is how the heartbreaking news is reported on the front page of the *Salem Gazette* under the headline, "Disaster strikes the ship Essex."

The news spreads quickly through the town, as well as to Boston and other nearby settlements. No house in Salem is unaffected by the incident, but there is one modest home sitting alone on a small hill that no one has yet reached with the news, and its owner cannot afford to buy the newspaper.

There are some people who deal with death as if it is a vicious rumor or a disaster that afflicts others, but never themselves. They do not realize that when death skips over them to touch others, it will eventually skip over others and come back to them. They think life is the converse of death, though it is an intrinsic part of it. Death is the foundation, life merely the incidental passerby. Death stands in wait of humans from the first day of life, allowing some relief while the newborn catches its first breath, and sometimes not even that much. Then it lies in wait behind every path and at every turn, every day and every month. It watches the human with a mischievous grin on its face. *Shall his appointed time be today or tomorrow?*

The woman in that house is holding a cup of coffee, looking out the kitchen window and watching her husband making repairs at their neighbor's house. She watches as their neighbor, Clark, emerges from his home with a newspaper in hand and calls out to Herman Paul to come down.

"Later. I'm rather busy at the moment," her husband answers from his perch atop the roof.

"This is more important," Clark answers.

From the kitchen window, her eyes follow her husband as he slowly descends the ladder.

He takes the newspaper from his neighbor's hand and reads the news of the ship that had transported his son. The newspaper drops from his hand, and he drops to his knees in apparent despair.

Clark approaches to try to embrace him.

Faith's heart sinks, and she rushes for the door.

Paul drops the tool in his hand to stand up, with the help of his neighbor, and slowly turns toward his house.

Faith is filled with dread as she rushes toward her husband. Her heart knows that something terrible has happened to her son.

With feet that feel like iron anvils, her husband drags himself towards her, and she unthinkingly takes a few steps backwards.

Three thousand miles away, to the south of Muscat and far out in the Indian Ocean, the ship with Captain Denault at the helm arrives in Mauritius. He soon learns that he has been summoned to testify before the French island's governor, General Decaen, about what happened to Captain Chapelain on the *Mihdhar*. What Captain Denault does not know is that some of the sailors who had worked on the *Mihdhar* and found themselves unemployed after Bin Aqeel dismissed them had found work on a French pirate ship headed for Mauritius before him. After landing on the French island, some of those sailors took to boasting about what they had seen while working on the *Mihdhar*. They spoke of how Chapelain had been killed when he refused to participate in the attack on the American ship *Essex*.

This news has prompted Decaen to summon Denault as soon as he learns of his arrival. Denault does not deny the account, and the governor swiftly puts Denault on trial on charges of failing to assist and protect his colleague. The French court rules that he should be incarcerated, despite Denault's defense that he'd had no hand in what happened to Chapelain. The fact that he had barely escaped being murdered himself isn't enough to get him off the hook. He had not only objected vociferously to Bin Aqeel's actions against the Americans in the heat of the moment, he explains, but was subsequently kept a prisoner in his cabin on the *Mihdhar*. Nevertheless, the court insists he could have done more to stop Bin Aqeel. After tossing Denault into jail, Decaen, in his capacity of General-in-Chief of the French Colonies in the East, issues a warrant for the arrest of Bin Aqeel for killing Captain Chapelain.

Thus, Bin Aqeel is now wanted by two major powers of the time, the English and the French, and faces refusal by local leaders in the surrounding regions. He is being pursued in all the places he used to frequent, with the exception of those controlled by Ibn Saud. He still sees the possibility of a helping hand in Ibn Saud, whom he had once tried to lend assistance against his enemy, the Sharif of Makkah.

Bin Aqeel settles into his old hometown of Mirbat, careful to stay in hiding now that word has filtered to him that he is wanted by both the English and the French authorities. His old allies and close friends among local influential people have deserted him. Even Al-Sharif Hamoud, the ruler of Abu Arish, who had once inclined toward the French interests in the Red Sea, has deserted him in favor of the British.

His one remaining non-hostile relationship, with Ibn Saud in Diriyah, makes him an outcast everywhere else. So, Bin Aqeel stays in Mirbat, proceeding to strengthen it with better management of local affairs. He develops trade activities in the city and builds some fortifications as a precaution against foreign attack, especially seaward.

He does not much like land travel and his personal sea journeys have become very limited. He doesn't dare venture far from Mirbat. Even so, he maintains a fleet of trade ships that continue to traverse the seas, trading in goods from one country to the next.

Bin Aqeel has often traded in horses and spices, and occasionally slaves, but the commodity most of his business focuses on now is export of *lubban*, frankincense, to the Far East. This is a trade the people of Mirbat have known for ages. The town's coastline and bays have also never failed to provide an abundance of fish and mollusks, which blesses Bin Aqeel and his family with additional revenues.

Enjoying quiet days after years of traveling the seas, the family experiences a brief period of harmony and stability. Sayyida Khadija continues to teach Abdullah, whom she now openly calls her son. The young boy is growing into a young man in Mirbat. His mother allows him to play barefoot in its streets, to race to the top of Samhan Mountain on outings, or to swim with his friends in the bays near their home, sometimes even to go fishing. He becomes fluent in Arabic and all of its local dialects, Shihri and Kathiri, as well as Mahri and a little Swahili. He also learns to recite the Qur'an eloquently and performs prayers with the Muslims at the prescribed times. Observers see no difference between him and the young men of Dhofar when noting his clothing, speech, or physique, except for the color of his eyes and his light skin, which constant exposure to the sun has turned almost bronze. He loves to mount one of his father's horses and ride bareback along the beach, sometimes taking off in a sprint to race another rider or just to challenge the wind.

Abdullah thrives in the home of Bin Aqeel under the care and tutelage of his adoptive parents. He has come to know no father other than Bin Aqeel and no mother other than Sayyida Khadija. His mother sees in him a good boy and holds great expectations for him. As she still has no living offspring of her own, Bin Aqeel begins to be truly convinced that this Christian child that he found one day on an American ship is becoming a Muslim son of his own family, one who might be of great help to him in his work.

Abdullah lives a simple life in his new home, as easy as the mellow ebb and flow of the waves on the shores of Mirbat, free of worries and distractions. Mirbat differs little from Salem in many ways. Both towns overlook the sea and are populated by robust, skilled sailors. Their ports, whose names are engraved on world maps, are connected with the globe, as is evident in their markets, where the displayed goods know no boundaries.

Yet in other ways, they are entirely different. Mirbat is an ancient Arabian town on the Arabian Sea and its people speak Arabic, with a legacy extending deep into the history of this place. In contrast, the American town is relatively new, having been established by some of the first Europeans to settle in the New World. It overlooks the Atlantic Ocean, and its people speak English.

Mirbat has made Abdullah forget Salem. He lives under the caring eye of his father, who is generous with his training and education, in addition to the lessons supervised by his mother. Sayyida Khadija does not want him to travel the seas, but the Sayyid convinces her to allow him to work on some of his ships sailing to nearby locations, such as Taqah and Salalah, so that he may learn the maritime arts, such as reading maps and navigation.

What most astonishes Abdullah is the *lubban*, the tree whose fragrant, resinous sap has left a luminous print on the history of Dhofar. For thousands of years, caravans sought out this precious commodity and brought it, as well as spices of the East, along the spice routes to the kings of Europe. It is said that urns full of _lubban_ were transported from the port of Samaharam in the Taqah region, just a few miles west of Mirbat, as gifts from Queen Bilqis of Sheba to the Prophet Solomon. As soon as spring arrives and temperatures begin to rise, the people start to scrape the *lubban* tree trunks, causing the sticky, fast-hardening liquid to ooze out. This is followed by a second and third round of scraping, like a surgical procedure on the tree's leg, causing it to shed tears that are collected and used as medicinal treatment for many ailments. What an amazing tree, muses Abdullah—its tears provide healing for human ailments!

Abdullah develops a passion for life and a love of discovery and knowledge, unmatched except by his father's passion for trade and love of possession and control. He benefits from his father's library, which contains books about history, religions, and peoples. He especially likes the history books and avidly reads about the ancient history of Dhofar; stories of *Shaddah bin Aad* and *Iram dhat al-'Imad*—the City of the Pillars—and what happened at *Al-Ahqaf*, the Sand Dunes, to the people of Prophet Hud, all of which are mentioned in the Qur'an.

The most significant part of settling in his new home is the atmosphere of amazement and discovery that envelops his life. He becomes intimately familiar with Arabian life in Mirbat. He is like a child who wakes up every day to see something new for the first time. Every day holds in store a new event, at home or in the stable or on the beach. It is as if he hears a new song for the first time every day, or discovers another world he has never lived in before. Slowly but surely, Abdullah forgets his ties to his past and becomes immersed in his present. Salem slips away and he becomes deeply connected to Mirbat.

But an ember remains burning in his heart, never quite winking out. It reminds him every time he wanders alone around the nearby bays and lagoons that he left a part of him somewhere else.

Bin Aqeel is not the type of person who can settle for a life of peace and quiet for long. After some time, he is longing for life on the sea once again, even though his ships are doing so on his behalf. His love of travel and craving to be the leader, always issuing orders, prompt him to bring the issue up with his wife. He knows she is content with their life in Mirbat, satisfied with their situation, so he thinks carefully of a way to break it to her.

He starts by recalling their stay in Muscat, how his business had been very profitable there, and goes on to say that he wishes to return to collect some outstanding debts, and that his business could go bankrupt if he does not collect those debts. She does not state a clear opinion on this, deferring to God's will in choosing what is best, as she always does. It's not her habit to give an opinion regarding her husband's business affairs unless he asks for it, but her eyes are turned toward Abdullah. She knows her husband will put him to work with him in his upcoming travels, which will not be like the small trips he took to Salalah or Taqah.

Bin Aqeel sends Abdullah to the master craftsman with whom he contracted to build a new ship, to urge him to speed up completion of the task. It has already been eight months since the two parties agreed on the terms to build the *sunbooq*, a type of dhow famous in those parts of Dhofar. Abdullah does not find the craftsman there, but he does meet with his primary apprentice, who informs him that the ship is almost ready. It will only be a few days until it is ready to sail.

The vessel, about sixty feet long, stands proudly over the beach, with its sharply pointed bow and squared-off stern. Carpentry tools are scattered around it—hammers, chisels, saws, and awls. Abdullah contemplates the solid construction, trying to locate the trace of a single nail used in building it, but he cannot. The *qallaf*, the boat-builder carpenter who implements the instructions of the master craftsman, reads Abdullah's expression of wonder. He proceeds to explain how the planks are lined up, then closely distributed holes are bored through the wood. The planks are then held firmly in place by ropes made of coconut fibers threaded through those holes. The holes are then covered with a mix of loofah fibers and cotton soaked in fish oil or coconut oil. It is said that the craftsmen and boat carpenters tend to have strong, healthy bodies and live long lives, thanks to a profession that trains their bodies with physical activity and patience.

All that remains to complete the *sunbooq* is decorating the stern of the vessel with patterns taken from Islamic designs or elegant motifs, especially flowers and leaves, to give the ship its own identity. Abdullah returns to inform his father that the carpenters have finished building the ship, which he decides to name *Al-Saqqoof*. Within a few short weeks, the *Saqqoof* is laden with fifty tons of various goods and departs Mirbat for Muscat to the north. Onboard is Bin Aqeel, his son Abdullah, and a group of sailors, in the first real voyage the Sayyid has taken since he retreated from the sailor's life.

Abdullah now stands at his father's side as an assistant. He is no longer the little boy in need of special care; he is now an adolescent, growing and strong enough to share in the sailors' work and even undertake the ship navigator's tasks and duties.

Bin Aqeel explains to his son why he chose to construct a *sunbooq*. He says that boats woven together by fibers are more flexible and safer when sailing in shallow waters and possibly colliding with rocks than those fastened together by iron nails. As for the type of lumber used in making the ship, it is teakwood brought from Calicut in India, as well as the gum Arabic tree and the Christ's Thorn jujube tree, both native to Oman.

Bin Aqeel continues to tell his son stories of the Omani people and the role they played since ancient times in maritime history. He speaks of how Oman lies at the junction of one of the most important sea routes linking India with the Gulf and on to the Red Sea and East Africa. It is also a key stop along the maritime Silk Route connecting Mesopotamia with the Far East in China. The journey begins at Al-Ubulla, near Basrah, and heads south by way of Bahrain, crosses through the Strait of Hormuz, and completes its course towards Ceylon, passing by Daibul at the mouth of the Indus River and southwards along the western coast of India. From there, the route turns east towards the Nicabur archipelago in the Bay of Bengal and on to Canton in South China. Another route stretches from Shatt al Arab, at the confluence of the Euphrates and Tigris rivers, to Sohar in Oman, then branches off in two directions. One goes southwest to Aden and the other seeks a southward course to the coast of Zanzibar in East Africa. There are other routes, too, such as the one connecting Aden with Palestine and Egypt, northwards through the Red Sea. The routes are many ... and the sea is one.

It is now the season of the forty-day chill of December 1809. The *Saqqoof* arrives in Muscat and anchors a short distance from the shore under dim, overcast skies. Bin Aqeel's men scan the channel to be sure there are no military vessels present belonging to the British Navy. The Sayyid is still on Bombay's wanted list. Once reassured of his situation, Bin Aqeel steps off his ship to visit some of the merchants who still owe him debts and tries to collect from them. He visits only two or three, getting a chilly reception. They try to stall on paying for goods he had sold them while living in Mirbat over the previous two years. His position is admittedly weak, since he is still being pursued by the English, but he feels that's no excuse for merchants in whom he had put his trust to treat him coldly.

He returns to his ship empty-handed to find Abdullah standing at the mast, taking in the view of the city that had welcomed him as a child, trying to remember the house they had lived in. Abdullah reads the signs of distress in his father's face as he mutters some unintelligible words and expletives.

"I trusted them and they let me down. That is the result of blind trust."

"Who do you mean, Father?"

"I thought those merchants were honest in their promises when I sold goods to them, but they betrayed me when it came time to pay."

"Did they deny that they owed you money?"

"No, and I don't think they will, because they know my friendly relationship with Al-Sayyid Saeed bin Sultan, and that I could complain about them if they denied it."

"So, what is bothering you?"

"Their procrastination. I don't know when we will recover our money. I had thought they were truthful to me."

"Life, my father, is not about people who seem to be truthful in front of you. Rather, it is about those who remain truthful when they are behind you."

Bin Aqeel is surprised by the wisdom in his son's last statement. He admires his maturity. Retiring to his cabin, he stretches out on his bed alone and contemplates the fate of their trip, initiated after such a long hiatus from the sea. He falls into slumber, feeling comforted about a decision he will leave for the morning sun.

Reenergized, Bin Aqeel rises early to wake his son before sunrise and instructs him to prepare for departure. Abdullah yawns sleepily and asks about the fate of the goods they brought with them, since they had not yet unloaded the *Saqqoof*. His father reveals his new plan: he has decided not to sell his merchandise in Muscat, but to take it somewhere else!

"But where to, Father?"

"To Basrah. We will sell our goods there."

"Basrah! You mean in Iraq?"

"Exactly."

"So when do we leave?" Abdullah asks again, barely opening his sleep-laden eyes.

"Tomorrow, since the wind is on our side."

Abdullah pulls himself up from his rest and proceeds to wash up and pray the dawn *fajr* prayer, while thick fog envelops their ship and leaves dewdrops resting on it in intricate patterns. His father calls him to have breakfast with him on the deck of the *Saqqoof*. He recalls the morning meal that his mother, Sayyida Khadija, would prepare for them: *aseedah*, a firm paste of cornmeal, sometimes mixed with millet or wheat, eaten with clarified butter and honey.

"I thought you would write to my mother to inform her of the change in course of our trip. She doesn't know that we are going farther on past Muscat."

"No need for that. I will tell her myself, since I will be returning to Mirbat," Bin Aqeel replies without raising his head.

"But ... I thought you said we're going to Basrah," Abdullah exclaims in surprise.

"*You* are going, not me!" Bin Aqeel responds with a smile, now gazing directly at his son's face, where traces of *aseedah* and butter are dripping down his chin.

"What? But ... I have no experience in trade, nor even in sailing!"

"As for the sea, don't forget you have spent more time on it and its shores than you have spent on land. And as for commerce, your attempt could not be worse than mine in collecting our debts here in Muscat."

There is no room for hesitation. He has made his decision, and there is no going back on it. What is certain is that he won't display any of the goods he brought from Mirbat in a market whose traders refuse to pay back their debts. Bin Aqeel believes that remaining in Muscat would be better for him than continuing on elsewhere. Here he can at least chase after those tardy debtors and try to collect whatever he can from them.

He also hopes to meet with Al-Sayyid Saeed bin Sultan to renew the past relationship and amicability between them. Bin Aqeel feels he needs to personally explain to the Sultan the reason he had to leave Muscat so abruptly. Who knows, maybe this visit will help him make amends with the Sultan and enable him to collect his debts with the traders of Muscat.

The *Saqqoof* sails away from Muscat towards the Strait of Hormuz on its way to Basrah. Onboard is Abdullah, sailing for the first time with no supervisor or guardian assigned to lead him. He is now the head of the ship. He bids his father farewell from the deck as the ship gently slips away from the channel. Bin Aqeel waves from the wharf, observing his son, once a boy playing with his friends in the alleys of Mirbat, now growing into a young man. Perhaps this is the opportunity he was waiting for, to test Abdullah and see the promise in him that his wife has so long believed in. He doesn't want to put too much hope in him—at least not yet. He has entrusted his first mate, Sayyida Khadija's maternal uncle, to navigate with Abdullah and be at his side as his assistant, leaving the decision-making regarding their journey up to the son.

The first mate notices Abdullah's uncertainty as Muscat disappears from sight and reassures him that this voyage will feel like a stone's throw away compared to his past experience journeying from America across the Atlantic Ocean. Abdullah responds that any trip is a stone's throw away compared to that one. The first mate advises him not to dwell on it, or even better, to not think at all.

"Remember that time is a journey on a single course. Once you are on board, it moves you along with no return, no going back to where you started. The pain and suffering become easier once you have the certainty they won't repeat themselves, because time is like a knot that loosens and unfurls before you in a straight line."

Abdullah finds some momentary comfort in these words, though he imagines that he might be too easily fooled. He may be like the one who endures the pain of a toothache, then goes numb.

After more thought, the first mate retracts his advice, because he will never succeed in not feeling pain.

"All I ask is that you imagine how time moves in a straight line, and know deep in your heart that once you have started a journey with pain, you have no choice but to come to the end. Know that everything will be fine in the end, and if it's not fine, it's not the end." Abdullah feels that he has heard these words somewhere before, but he does not know where.

The Gulf of Oman narrows as the *Saqqoof* approaches the Strait of Hormuz and enters a snug passageway of no more than thirty-one miles across. Passing by the last tip of the strait, the ship enters the waters of the Persian Gulf, which is relatively shallow in comparison with the Gulf of Oman. Now, they are passing along one of the oldest maritime routes in the world, which the earliest human sailors first navigated.

Abdullah recalls his father telling him the story of a kingdom that became famous for its commerce and wealth and was established right here on Hormuz Island and the adjacent shore around four centuries earlier. This kingdom's reach and power spread from Al-Qatif in the north to Julfar in the east, on the Arabian coast of the Persian Gulf. The Venetian explorer Marco Polo mentioned it when he related how ships laden with spices, silk fabrics, and ivory from India came to sell their goods in this kingdom's markets, whose tradesmen then distributed these wares all over the world. It is said to have been established by an Arabian shaykh from Oman, possibly from Yemen, who went to Persia to build an Arabic-speaking city that became one of the most important trade markets in the world, before its later demise at the hands of the Portuguese.

The region is tranquil at dawn, before the north winds whip up some lofty waves in the cold December air, pushing the ship in a southwest direction as it lilts and sways to the rhythmic group chants of the men, in Abdullah's ears not unlike the shanties sung by New England sailors, as they tug the sails up the mast. "O Allah, O Allah ... we say O Allah ... *hoo low*, my master, *hoo low*, oh fear of Allah."

Then the winds die down, allowing the *Saqqoof* to glide along a surface that is now a glossy mirror, in air saturated with a light fog. Abdullah draws his cloak tightly around him against the cold, enjoying the sailor's chant that stirs in him a longing for places he left as a child that he barely remembers now. Songs and voices and pictures, even smells, can sometimes take a person back to a single still moment in time. That moment can arise merely by hearing a tune that one never paid attention to in the past, or by seeing a sight, or smelling a passing scent. Then it suddenly jumps into view, evoking a whole chain of memories.

Now that Abdullah has opened his bottle of memories, he will have to accept what pours out of it, sweet honey or bitter melon, even though the honey will drip quickly out of his hands, while the latter lasts much longer. He tries to recall his childhood days, grasping any image he can envision of his hometown of Salem, its port, wharf, and people, and the mother and father he left behind there. Does he remember his mother?

He does not remember much about her besides a few glimpses that pass through his mind like flashes of light. He tries to slow these flickers down, to get a better picture in his mind's eye of the shape of her eyes, the roundness of her face, and the feel of her lips when she plants a kiss on his forehead at bedtime.

The first mate notices his distraction and asks him to watch the bow of the ship, especially in this murky weather. He advises him, "Some memories are better left as is."

Could this be true? Abdullah asks himself. *Is it better to leave memories alone? No, this is not right.*

Abdullah tries to recall whatever he can before it is lost to time again. He knows he cannot relive those memories, so why not preserve what remains of them?

The first mate warns him again that reminiscing might be easy, but forgetting is difficult. Memories are like bullets that suddenly shower down without you realizing it. Some pass by like lightning, making you shudder and tremble. Others will kill you.

Abdullah contemplates the thick fog around him. The things he remembers in this moment seem more real than what his senses perceive. The men continue in their chant, "O Allah, O Allah ... we say O Allah ... *hoo low*, my master, *hoo low*, oh fear of Allah."

After a few days of sailing in overcast weather interspersed with rain, they modify *Saqqoof's* course and head northwest. They are deep within the Persian Gulf, but a peninsula can be seen from the port side of the boat. Abdullah asks if this is Qatar. His assistant confirms it as the ship passes it by and turns left again, towards Bahrain.

Abdullah notices concern in his assistant's eyes, as the sailors whisper among them that they are in the vicinity of the Rahmah bin Jaber fleet. Rahmah is notorious for raiding trade ships and looting all they have to fund his campaign against his cousins in the family of Aal Khalifah, in their dispute over Bahrain. The first mate is aware that Rahmah currently has an accord with the Sultan of Oman, which might help protect them, but Rahmah switches alliances wherever the changing winds take his interests.

Furthermore, he is wary of attacking any ship that raises the British flag, or harming any British subjects. Since Bin Aqeel is wanted by the British, his ship would be up for grabs for Rahmah, a man known to be fierce and cruel with whoever was caught in his trap.

The *Saqqoof* sways as it sails nimbly over the water's surface, rushing to escape this dangerous region. Abdullah's assistant points to Khor Hassan, at the northernmost tip of Qatar, where Rahmah's fleet, manned by hundreds of loyal men and their families, is based. The ship continues along its risky course and heads for Bahrain, where they stop to resupply their drinking water and move on. In ancient times, these watery regions to the north and east of Bahrain were known for the best pearl beds in the world, since the sea's depth runs to no more than twenty to thirty yards. Abdullah is careful to avoid the small islands scattered across their path, while admiring the flat surface of nearly white sand on the sea bottom, visible through these crystal-clear waters.

"Do you know, Abdullah, that the pearl trade is worth half a million rupees in these islands? Most of it goes to Surat, Calcutta, and Malabar, from where it is distributed throughout India and China," says his assistant. "Some of it goes to Mokha, where you came from, whence it moves on to European markets and ends up on the neck of a princess living in a palace." Abdullah is impressed at his assistant's broad knowledge. He hasn't paid much attention to this before, even though he has seen him almost every week with Bin Aqeel in their home in Mirbat, as if he was one of the family.

The *Saqqoof* draws closer to the western side of the Persian Gulf adjoining the Arabian Peninsula, enabling Abdullah to view a shore lined with palm trees. His assistant points to this area as the Al-Qatif Oasis and explains that these lands, as far as the eye can see, are controlled by Ibn Saud, whose power base is in Diriyah, in the land of Najd.

Bin Aqeel's first mate navigates while Abdullah practices using the *kamal* navigation device, a flat, carved piece of wood with a small rope hanging from the center, to determine the ship's latitudinal location and its course. Abdullah holds the rope between his teeth, such that the bottom of the *kamal* is in line with the horizon, while the top of it is in line with a clearly identified star in the sky. From there, he identifies their location by tying a knot in the rope. When he has free time, he reviews the book *Advantages of the Rules of Maritime Sciences* by Ibn Majid, which he had read with his teachers in Mirbat.

Sailors are no different from each other in any part of the world. They share the same convictions. They are optimistic about the same things and pessimistic about the same things. They even share similar practices, probably ever since mankind invented sails to harness the wind.

The *Saqqoof* arrives at Al-Faw, where the estuary of Shatt al-Arab pours into the Persian Gulf, completing its journey within a narrow canal of Iraqi waters passing by the land of the Ahwaz peoples, the homeland of the Arab tribe of Bani Kaab. The first mate leaves the helm to Abdullah so that he can focus on maneuvering the ship through the mouth of the river and measuring the water's depths to determine a safe course of passage. The estuary continues for about thirty-five miles before the *Saqqoof* can reach Basrah, where palm trees line the shores as if standing to welcome guests arriving from afar.

Abdullah gives his orders to the sailors to raise the sail on the smallest styliform mast, taking advantage of the strong winds to push the ship northwestward. In a few short hours, the ship and its crew find themselves in Basrah, known as the Treasury of Literature. The *Saqqoof* drops anchor in the harbor at the end of a trip that has lasted less than three weeks.

Now Abdullah can disembark and sell his father's merchandise in the markets of Basrah, being paid in cash in the form of French riyals, also known as Maria Theresa thalers. It doesn't take long to unload the goods, so he decides to spend the rest of his day visiting the city's historic sights, the likes of which he has not seen in the cities he visited in Oman or Yemen. His assistant suggests they visit the shops of Nahr al-Banat and Al-Doogh that lie at the end of the marketplace.

Surrounding the city is a perimeter wall built of adobe bricks, further encircled by a narrow moat on the north, east, and south sides and land on the west side, where it faces the desert. Abdullah enters through Bab Al-Ribat, one of the city's five gates, and heads for the marketplace. He wanders among tens of shops, the likes of which he has never seen before in his life. Thousands of people throng the city's roads and narrow alleyways. Its canals infiltrate the palm groves that stretch for long distances from the estuary, astonishing him with their intricate network of tributaries and abundant flow of water. The canals are packed with small boats whose owners shout when they bump against each other. *No need to rush*, Abdullah says to himself. *Look at the river; it knows that it will reach its destination in the end.*

He continues on to the market, where hundreds of kinds of goods are on display for a strange mix of buyers: Persians, Turks, Armenians, and Indians, as well as Arabs and a few Europeans. He reaches the shop called Nahr al-Banat that his assistant had suggested to him. There he finds the shopkeeper berating a poor, disheveled boy for standing too long in front of his store. He is telling him not to come back unless he brings some dust from heaven, hoping he'll be distracted with such a task and not bother him.

Abdullah watches with interest as the poor boy walks away broken, then stops momentarily in front of a woman in a billowing cloak. He speaks to her for a few seconds, as if asking her something, and as soon as she moves away, he scoops up some of the dust she was standing on. He brings it back to the shopkeeper, rolled in the end of his sleeve, saying, "Here is what you asked for. That woman is a mother, and this comes from under her feet."[1] The shopkeeper bursts into tears at the boy's words and gives him whatever he pleases.

Abdullah's eyes tear up as he observes this incident and recalls his mother in Salem, again trying to keep her image in his mind's eye before it disintegrates and vanishes. He buys some clothing for his mother Khadija and is moved to buy a gift for her young maidservant, Salma, who caught his attention when he first arrived in Mirbat.

He got to know her in the Sayyid's home; often they would go down to the beach to play together. Like him, she knew very little about her Balushi parents, because she had been kidnapped from her village on the other side of the Persian Gulf and sold at a young age. But Sayyida Khadija bought her and freed her to stay working in their large home, along with many other workers. Sayyida Khadija allowed them to play together on the nearby beach, where they romped barefoot among the waves or searched for birds' nests within the rocks to bring eggs back home with them.

There is no sight that prompts a feeling of freedom and gushing energy more than two children running with the wind along a beach, hands reaching out as if they are two birds with wings spread, soaring high in the sky. As Abdullah grew, his feelings have matured toward the girl who he had once teased by pulling on her curly locks of hair, making her drop the eggs from her hands and chase after him on the sandy shore.

Abdullah continues on to the next clothing shop and stops to buy some gifts for his father. There is such a variety of goods here, displayed in ways he has never seen before. He finds the Yemeni coffee from Mokha and Hudaydah that he knew well. He feels the exquisite texture of pure silk and the scent of tea brought from China. There are foods such as rice, sugar, and oils, as well as cotton, rugs, and spices. Even the pearls from the famous Bahrain pearl-divers have a share in the displays, but what takes the lion's share of sales is the trade in dates for which Basrah is famous, followed by horses and slaves.

Before setting sail for home, he buys some food and gifts to give his assistant and the ship's crew, to show his appreciation for their role in this journey that has garnered copious profits and is certain to please his father when he returns, as he had hoped. He recalls his father's words, that the difference between one journey and another is not in the type of vessel, but the type of passengers.

Chapter Six

Once Abdullah has left Muscat, his father moves quickly to follow up on collecting unpaid debts and extracting whatever he can from those who remain delinquent. He also pays a cordial visit to Al-Sultan Saeed in his palace. The Sultan does not ask him to explain his long absence, but Bin Aqeel feels it is only befitting to apologize to the Sultan for his sudden departure and offers an adequate explanation for that.

Bin Aqeel can't shake the agony of being chased by the English and, by extension, does not want to discomfit the few allies with whom he still has strong ties. To this end, he decides to send a letter to the governor of Bombay, Jonathan Duncan, explaining his situation. He begins by apologizing for leasing Kamaran to the French. In his letter, Bin Aqeel requests that the British government halt its pursuit of him and permit him to move freely and reside in lands and waters controlled by the British. He knows the letter is quite a long shot but figures it won't hurt to try. His past acquaintance with Duncan might help get him off the hook, at least a little.

At to the remaining unpaid debts, Bin Aqeel tries compromise. Some he allows more time to pay, and from some he accepts a smaller amount, to speed up the process. He reconciles himself to his loss with the aphorism, "Getting to halfway sets you free." After finishing his daily rounds, Bin Aqeel stops by the wharf to watch a while for Abdullah's return from Basrah. He has started to long for him as if the boy were his own flesh and blood.

Two weeks after Abdullah's departure, Bin Aqeel is sitting on the wharf when his assistant approaches with a letter that has arrived from Luhayya, via Mirbat. He unfolds it to discover that it is from his old ally Al-Sharif Hamoud, the ruler of Abu Arish, asking his help to obtain some weapons and ammunition and to buy a large ship and bring it to Luhayya with a hired captain as soon as possible.

Bin Aqeel recollects his last encounter with Al-Sharif Hamoud, years ago now, when he bought Kamaran. He remembers that Al-Sharif had not stipulated at the time what he would be permitted do with the island, nor had he placed any restrictions on his management of the island in the sales agreement and receipt of payment. What happened later was the result of meddling by an outside party. If not for Pringle's tattling and interference, his relationship with Al-Sharif Hamoud would not have gone bad.

Nevertheless, he reads between the lines of the letter, seeing in it Al-Sharif's desire to revive their previous relationship. Why would Al-Sharif ask him to obtain some weapons and other gear if he did not wish to open a new page of friendship between them?

Bin Aqeel ponders what might have caused Al-Sharif to request such weaponry. He's aware of the ongoing dispute between Al-Sharif and his rivals in the region, such as the imam of Yemen and even Ibn Saud, but he has not heard of any current battles among those parties. He decides to comply with the request and sends a letter to his brother Abdulrahman, in Mokha, to let him know that he will be passing by to visit him very soon.

Bin Aqeel could find no better ship than the one owned by Al-Sultan Saeed. The *Falak* is a common type of merchant sailing ship used in the region called a *xebec*, or *boum* in the local Omani dialect. He had seen it anchored in the port with a palace guard on board who allowed him to take a tour of it.

An idea sparks in his mind as he finishes reading Al-Sharif's letter. He has enough money to purchase the xebec but barely enough to cover the cost of building one like it, and he can't wait months for such construction to be completed.

He decides to offer the Sultan an amount he can't refuse, knowing from the guard that the ship has not sailed for quite some time, suggesting that Al-Sultan doesn't need it. To guarantee Al-Sultan's agreement, he offers him a tantalizing amount equal to the cost of two new xebecs. He will pay the first half immediately, while the remainder will be left for the Sultan to collect from Bin Aqeel's debtors in Muscat. In this way, he gets what he wants instantly and ends his pursuit of his debtors, or rather, transfers the task of collecting to Al-Sultan, who will surely know better how to extract payment from his subjects.

The deal is sealed as Bin Aqeel wished; actually, even better. He is also able to convince the Sultan to loan him some money until his son returns. He uses this cash to procure some of the weapons and ammunition that Al-Sharif had requested, keeping this purpose secret from Al-Sultan Saeed and avoiding arousing anyone's suspicion.

Three weeks after the purchase of the *Falak*, news comes late one afternoon that the *Saqqoof* has returned. Bin Aqeel rushes to greet his son. The news is all good, and Bin Aqeel congratulates him on his safe return and successful voyage, during which he was able to sell all the merchandise he sent with him. Bin Aqeel has been in great need of a profitable deal to renew his confidence after seeing his business falter.

Abdullah relates to his father all that he saw on this journey through the Strait of Hormuz to Shatt al-Arab, how he was able to sail the ship himself through such narrow waters, and how he sold all of the goods in the markets of Basrah at an ample profit. The young man's eyes glisten with pride and confidence in himself as he describes the journey and how he evaded the pirate ships of Rahmah bin Jabir at Khor Hassan, and of Basrah and how much he marveled at the city. He speaks of how he steered the ship himself and managed the affairs of the crew, not hiding his pride in all his successes.

Bin Aqeel contemplates his son's animated face as he speaks. At that moment, he realizes Abdullah has become just what Sayyida Khadija predicted; he is worthy of being their son. Sayyida Khadija, of course, has never needed proof of her son's worth. Her feelings for him sprang from the heart, and the love she gave him from the first day she set eyes on him was unconditional. Since when does a mother's devotion to her child need explanation?

Bin Aqeel shows the letter from Al-Sharif to his son and informs him that he will answer his old ally's request. He says this may benefit them, especially because he is still wanted by both the British and the French. Abdullah does not remember Al-Sharif Hamoud well, but the names of places like Luhayya and Kamaran bear both pleasant and painful memories that hang weightily in his mind.

Thanks to the abundant funds Abdullah brought with him from Basrah, Bin Aqeel hurries to fulfill Al-Sharif's requests. The next day, he begins seeking a captain for the *Falak*, ultimately choosing a Frenchman, Nicola, who has been looking for work in Muscat.

Even now, he maintains a preference for the Frenchmen he has worked with in the past, having come close to establishing a representative of their government in Mauritius on Kamaran. But he is averse to the British, not feeling safe in the face of their deceitfulness. Besides, some of the French will work freelance even if they are affiliated with the French navy. They can be found traversing the Indian Ocean as local pirates on midsized schooners with two sails, called *batteel* in the local dialect. Sometimes they operate under the umbrella of the French government, but others are fugitives from its service, which makes it possible to negotiate with them directly.

The sailors Bin Aqeel has hired load what they can of the lightweight weapons and ammunition he has purchased on the *Falak*, still floating idle in Muscat's port. Before leaving, Bin Aqeel returns to the Sultan to bid farewell and repay back the loan with words of gratitude, now that his son's success has brought him the funds he needed.

The *Falak* sets sail with Bin Aqeel and Captain Nicola on board, followed by the *Saqqoof* bearing Abdullah and the rest of the sailors, and heads south to pass by Mirbat. Here the *Saqqoof* will stay, with Abdullah transferring to the *Falak* to complete the voyage with his father. They make a brief stop to visit Sayyida Khadija and allow Abdullah to present the gifts he brought her from Basrah. The Sayyida is overjoyed to hear the news of their successes in Muscat and Basrah and offers a prayer for their prosperity in future endeavors. She feels reassured and ready to settle down in her home.

She has worked so hard to take in the young boy, to bring him up and educate him to become a man of the house of Al-Sayyid, a son they can depend on. Her reward is seeing her husband truly becoming a father to Abdullah. Abdullah excuses himself from this happy reunion to greet Salma and give her the gift he chose from the Nahr al-Banat shop in Basrah, taking a few moments to read her eyes and confirm her feelings for him before he says goodbye.

The *Falak* departs Mirbat once Bin Aqeel is reassured that his wife has given her blessing to this venture towards Al-Sharif, since he has much faith in her wisdom.

The ship remains close to the coast as it sails through the Arabian Sea, stopping at some ports to purchase more weapons and supplies, until it reaches Aden. The last time Bin Aqeel set foot here was few years before, when he made his unsuccessful attempt to communicate with the sultan of Lahj at his residence in Yafea. He tries again this time and sends his messenger across Wadi Tuban towards Al-Hawta, north of Aden, the capital of the Abdali clan. Abdullah remembers arriving in Aden on the *Essex*, the first Arab land where he heard the *azan*, the call to prayer, from minarets, but he does not remember staying in the city. Bin Aqeel's messenger to the sultan of Lahj returns with an unfavorable answer, still refusing to accept a visit from him, so the *Falak* raises its anchor and continues on its course to Luhayya.

The *Falak* enters the strait of Bab al-Mandab by way of the narrow Bab Iskandar strait, no more than two miles wide between the coast of Yemen and the island of Mayyun, with rather shallow waters that force the ship to travel quite slowly. Captain Nicola points to the island of Mayyun on the port side and tells Abdullah how the French had controlled it about six decades before, when they first arrived in this region, but then lost it to the English, represented by the East India Company. Consequently, the French turned their eyes to another island, Kamaran, which differed from Mayyun in that it possessed fresh water sources. Kamaran's ample water would be needed to establish a colony. "And you know the rest of the story, Abdullah."

He has just finished his words when a frightened gasp from one of the new sailors interrupts the conversation. He has dropped a box into the sea that held the Sayyid's personal porcelain tea set as he was carrying it to the Sayyid's cabin. No one speaks a word of the incident to the Sayyid, but Bin Aqeel's ear catches the sound. Nevertheless, he shows no anger to the novice sailor.

The *Falak* continues sailing northwards to reach the coffee-trade capital of Mokha. Bin Aqeel is well aware that the British representative maintains an office in Mokha and has eyes throughout the port and nearby waters. He asks Captain Nicola to reduce their speed before entering the harbor, to lower the mainsail and raise the smaller one normally used in high winds, to avoid being noticed. The *Falak* slows as it reaches the harbor's southern end and comes to a stop, dropping anchor just outside the harbor. Off the port side, the sun appears to sink into the waters of the Red Sea, heralding the end of another day in the month of February 1810.

Bin Aqeel notices foreign trade ships lined up with Arabian cargo ships of many types: *sunbooq* (dhow), *jalboot* (jolly boat), *shoo'ee* (small sailboat), and the large-sized *baghla*. With Captain Nicola's help, he is able to distinguish the identities of the flags flying from the masts of the foreign ships. Some are Dutch or Portuguese, two French, in addition to a few small fishing boats.

It is not unusual to see foreign boats here in Mokha. The port's fame has reached all corners of the earth, via vessels bearing from it the finest coffee, incense, and raisins. Mokha has long had a global appearance, as the Franciscan Catholic missionary Remedius Prutky wrote when he visited this city five decades before the arrival of the *Falak*. Prutky came here from Massawa, on the other side of the Red Sea, when the Ethiopian Emperor Iyasu II banished him on the advice of his Coptic archbishop. The missionary wrote that Mokha was a place of great ethnic diversity, where one could hear various languages spoken in its markets. He was amazed to see lodging for travelers and strangers in the form of large homes for rent, some containing at least one hundred rooms. There was no distinction or discrimination based on origin, color, or religion as to who could rent a room.

Bin Aqeel casts a look around the port in search of any English military ships. Not finding any, he breathes a sigh of relief. The two French cargo ships do not concern him, but he does overlook one foreign ship anchored at the edge of the harbor, raising a flag neither he nor Captain Nicola is familiar with.

Bin Aqeel orders Captain Nicola to bring the ship closer into the harbor once he feels safe from British detection. The *Falak* reaches the port entrance, which comprises two narrow, bow-shaped passageways, finally dropping anchor near the mysterious unidentified ship. Bin Aqeel has dinner with Abdullah and retires to his cabin aboard the *Falak,* expecting a contented night's sleep, with the unknown ship just twenty or thirty yards away.

Abdullah sits awake that evening, contemplating the view of the city under the dome of a clear sky. The full moon reflects off the water to illuminate the wharf. Voices coming from the ship nearby catch his attention. He hears some words in English he has not forgotten. The accent reminds him of the family he left behind. The ship also seems familiar to him in its design and build, and the flag it has raised on its mast is not unfamiliar to him.

What Abdullah does not know is that this ship is American. Not just that, but it belongs to the family of Orne, who owned the *Essex*, the ship Bin Aqeel burned down years before at Kamaran and whose captain and crew he had ordered killed and tossed into the sea.

In the early morning, Bin Aqeel orders a small boat to be lowered to transport him and two assistants to the shore. Abdullah and Captain Nicola remain with the rest of the crew on the *Falak*. Bin Aqeel enters Bab al-Sahil to pass through the ancient city towards the house of his brother Abdulrahman, while storekeepers begin to open their doors to a new work day. The market perimeter gradually swells with people, producing a mixed hubbub of sellers pitching their wares and livestock being herded toward roads out of town. Some sellers begin with a daily recitation of the Qur'an, while others repeat morning supplications, asking God to bestow His bounties upon them, before they call out to potential customers and shoppers, boasting the virtues of the goods they have brought from the nearby mountainous regions.

Bin Aqeel continues on, passing by huts built of straw, until he reaches Al-Shadhili Mosque, with its nine domes. He stops momentarily to look around him, then asks his assistants to wait while he proceeds to the central court of the mosque to offer a short prayer near the niche that indicates the *qibla*, the correct direction for prayer. Overhead, the walls, arches, and ceilings are decorated with geometrical motifs that frame Qur'anic verses, all artfully carved out of gypsum plaster. The mosque is nearly empty at this time of the morning, save a few worshippers gathered at the southern side, under the dome and near the tomb of the mosque's builder.

In this cubical building under its dome lie the remains of Shaykh Al-Shadhili, who is said to have discovered coffee, in addition to other wonders for which innocent-minded people credit him. Some say a trader came from India to Mokha after the winds changed his Jiddah-bound ship's course. Onboard was the trader's son, who was very ill. The ship's passengers caught sight of a lone hut in a desolate area. The trader and some of the passengers carried his sick child to the hut, hoping the occupant could provide some help, though most assumed this attempt would be in vain. The hut's occupant welcomed them into his humble home, which was simply furnished with a straw mat for sleeping and a table for preparing food. The trader asked where the rest of his furnishings were.

The man replied, "My condition is no better than yours, my friend. I don't see you having any furnishings, either!" The trader replied, astonished, "But I am just a traveler," to which the man in the hut exclaimed, "And so am I!" He offered a warm drink to the sick person, who, as soon as he took a few sips, began to feel better. Once the trader was comforted that his son would recover, the man in the hut asked him to display his goods at the nearby village market, which he pointed out was brimming with Indians and Yemenis selling their merchandise. He told him this drink would reach across the world.

News of the man in the hut spread, and people came from all over to see him and purchase the trader's now-famous commodity. As the story goes, the trader returned to India to inform his friends and came back with ships loaded with merchandise to trade in Mokha for coffee to be carried to the rest of the world. The man in the hut was none other than Al-Shadhili, and the village none other than Mokha.

A woman sits with her cloak wrapped around her, beneath the minaret at the northeastern corner of the mosque. She watches Bin Aqeel as he leaves the center of the mosque, staring at him as if in disbelief. She takes another look, as if trying to be sure of what she sees, before continuing on her way. Bin Aqeel moves on with his assistants until he reaches his brother's house and spends the rest of the day with him.

His brother, who has been expecting his arrival any day now, welcomes him warmly and settles in to relate the news he missed while living far away over the past few years—news of the land of Yemen and neighboring land of Al-Mikhlaf Al-Sulaymani, the territory that extends north from Hudaydah and includes Luhayya, towards Jizan and Abu Arish. Bin Aqeel is interested in news mainly about the movements and actions of Al-Sharif Hamoud, even more than his concerns about his English pursuers and far more than the whereabouts of the French. He wants to know what Al-Sharif intends to do and what prompted him to dismiss their feud and ask for his help in supplying arms and ammunition.

Bin Aqeel is aware that Al-Sharif Hamoud is now subject to the rule of Ibn Saud, after his defeat a few years earlier by Abdulwahhab Al-Mutahami, the Saudi deputy known as Abu Nuqta. Falling under the rule of Diriyah was a temporary tactic for Al-Sharif; clashes between the two sides in fact continued without stop. The third party in the regional power equation was the Imam of Yemen, Ali bin Abbas, who played a role in the conflict on the borders of his territory. Al-Sharif tried to take control of Hudaydah, which was governed at the time by the *faqih* (judge) Salih Al-Ulufi under the Imamate, but he failed when Al-Ulufi took shelter in an impregnable fort and they ended up reconciling. Bin Aqeel recalls how he mediated between the two at the time.

At a place not far from the wharf in Mokha's port, near Bab Sandalwood, sits a small office maintained by the American Agency. Prominent American traders established this office recently, in coordination with their country's government, to manage their interests in the region and represent them in negotiations for purchasing goods, especially with the surge in coffee exports to the North Atlantic. The resident officer is conferring with Captain Beckman, the captain of the American ship anchored in the harbor, reviewing the ship's next stop in Hudaydah in pursuit of the city's high-quality coffee. Their discussion is interrupted by shouting, and a guard dashes in to tell the officer that a woman is at the door, insisting on meeting with him.

Receiving permission to enter, the woman comes through the door apprehensively, apparently afraid of something. Her words are hurried, as if she is being chased. The agency officer can't make out what she's saying, though he is familiar with the local Arabic dialect used here in the Tihama region. He asks her to slow down. She is waving in the direction of the port, shrieking something about an American boy being here, and seeing the man who kidnapped him when he was a little boy just now leaving Al-Shadhili Mosque.

The agency officer thinks she surely must be insane, especially when she continues repeating this bizarre tale of an American child kidnapped on a ship right there in the port. Her clothing and general appearance suggest she is a beggar, so he orders the guard to remove her from his office. The woman struggles as she is led out, trying to stay put, but the guard pulls her out, still babbling, and the two Americans return to their work.

Suddenly, the word "*Essex*" reaches the ears of the American captain as the woman speaks it outside. The pen in the captain's hand drops to the table as he looks at the officer to verify if he heard the same word. The man nods. How could a poor woman from Tihama know about the *Essex*?

The officer immediately tells the guard to let her back in. He invites her to sit down and asks her to speak calmly and relate what she knows about the *Essex*. This time, they listen to her seriously. She tells them what she knows of the *Essex's* fate, and how there was a survivor kidnapped by Bin Aqeel. He was just a boy then, and she saw him with her own eyes in the lodging of Bin Aqeel's wife on Kamaran, the scene of the treachery that befell the fated ship.

This woman is none other than Zainab, Sayyida Khadija's friend and companion since childhood, who had long harbored a jealousy of her marriage to Al-Sayyid Bin Aqeel. Zainab had accompanied Sayyida Khadija on the trip from Kamaran to Muscat, but returned to Mokha after the death of her husband. She had hoped to find someone from her husband's family there, but they had all passed away and she was left to survive on charity from people visiting the tomb of Al-Shadhili.

The news of a survivor from the *Essex* comes as a shock to Captain Beckman, who works for the Orne family and knows of the ship's fate. He doesn't think anyone in Salem knew of such a survivor, either. The agency officer knows nothing of this. There have been rumors, but nothing of this nature had been documented by the British administrator, and the only witness, Haidar, had left Mokha when he feared repercussions.

By midday, Bin Aqeel wraps up his visit with his brother, after gleaning as much news as he can about Al-Sharif Hamoud. He returns to the *Falak* thinking that his stop in Mokha has gone unnoticed by the British.

Meanwhile, the American Agency officer and American captain hurry to the office of the British administrator to consult with him on Zainab's revelations. Pringle having been transferred to an office in India, the acting administrator is now a Captain Redland, who is hesitant to believe the story but agrees to investigate the matter. Bin Aqeel is, after all, still a wanted man. Redland doesn't recall any report left by his predecessor mentioning a child survivor from the *Essex*. But there is another way to determine the woman's truthfulness: go to the vessel she purported to be Bin Aqeel's ship and speak with its owner directly. Redland has limited capacity to pressure Bin Aqeel if he discovers the story is true; the nearest British military force is hundreds of miles away. But he does have the political authority to mobilize some local forces to arrest Bin Aqeel, or so he believes.

Before the sun sets, a small boat launches from the port bearing three men headed for the anchored *Falak*. One of the Sayyid's servants notices the boat coming toward them, carrying what looks like the

British administrator and two other men. Bin Aqeel, alerted to the visitors, takes a position at the stern where he will have a clear view of the deck. He orders Abdullah to retreat to his cabin and lock the door. Abdullah is perplexed by this demand; he's not a little boy to be ordered about this way anymore. But the insistence in Bin Aqeel's tone prompts him to obey. The boat arrives at the *Falak,* and its passengers request permission to board. Captain Nicola glances at the Sayyid's face for a sign, and he gestures to allow them aboard.

A rope ladder is lowered from the deck. Captain Redland is the first to use it to climb up, followed by the American Agency officer and Captain Beckman. The latter, thwarting Redland's attempt at discretion, has become agitated thinking of the terrible fate of the *Essex* and begins badgering the crew: "Where is the owner of the ship? Where is he? Come on! Bring him out now!"

But as soon as all three are standing on the ship's deck, they find themselves confronted by a tough-looking gang of muscular sailors. The American captain calms down a bit and softens his tone.

"Who do you think you are, boarding our ship and raising your voice like that!? And who are you in the first place?" Captain Nicola asks in French-accented English, directing his words to the American captain.

"I do apologize for my colleague's hot-headed behavior," says the British captain, casting a disapproving look at the American. "I am Captain Redland, the British administrator in Mokha. I would like to speak with the ship's owner, if I may."

Captain Nicola glances surreptitiously at the face of the Sayyid sitting at the stern of the ship, who signals him to keep talking.

"And what do you want from him?" Nicola asks.

"It is a personal matter between us," Redland answers while making a point of examining some boxes stacked onboard.

"Can I help you?"

"I don't think so," Redland replies, buying time. He surveys the faces of the watching sailors, as if looking for something specific. He knows some Arabic and tries to make out what they are whispering to each other.

"But I am the captain of the ship," Nicola retorts.

Redland notices the lid on one of the boxes has slipped aside. He pretends to trip so as to lean over and take a look, and catches a glimpse of the arms stored inside the box.

At that same moment, Abdullah sneaks a peek from behind Bin Aqeel's cabin and wonders, *What made my father forbid me from seeing them?*

"Fine, then. Since you are the captain, how about you tell me more about the white-skinned boy of European or American origin who is working on your ship?"

Taken aback, Nicola hesitates. Bin Aqeel, alarmed, jumps down from his vantage point and walks briskly up to the visitors, hand on the dagger in his belt and five of his toughs close behind, and faces Captain Redland directly.

"I am the owner of the ship. What is it you want from us?"

Redland contemplates the man in front of him. Could this be the man who killed Captain Carter and disposed of his body in the sea, then slayed the American crew and burnt their ship, to become wanted and pursued by the British government?

"You did not register your ship in the port registry. Are you not aware that all ships must register here?"

"I know this, but I am not carrying goods for Mokha, and I don't intend to use the port services."

"Fine, then, you may certainly do that, but you have not told me your name."

"I am Al-Sayyid Muhammad Bin Aqeel Al-Saqqaf, and this is my captain, Captain Nicola."

"You ... you are Al-Sayyid Muhammad Bin Aqeel?"

"In the flesh."

Redland pauses for a moment to catch his breath. His picture of the man until now has been of a hulking, ugly beast, his eyes sparking evil, or possibly a one-eyed pirate wearing a tricorne hat with a feather in the band. But here stands an average-looking Arab, on the short side and a bit portly, neatly attired and apparently attentive to good grooming and elegant clothing. Redland takes a few steps back and gestures to his companions to return to their small boat. His position and lack of military muscle do not permit him to give orders here, nor does he have the means to inspect the vessel to search what he is looking for. The three return quietly to their boat, uncertain as to how to confront Bin Aqeel's men.

That evening, Captain Nicola goes quietly to Abdullah and presses him hard to tell him his story of how he came to be in this land, and his real name. Abdullah reluctantly relates his story, eliciting deep sympathy in the captain, who had never dared ask such questions of the young man until now. He starts thinking about ways that Abdullah might quickly steal away to the American ship anchored within a short distance from *Falak*, so he can return to his family in America.

At first, Abdullah is excited about Nicola's plan and spends the next hour bundling up his things to prepare to leave. But at the last moment, he hesitates. His heart wells up with conflicting emotions, tossing him right and left like his own ship on a stormy day. On the one hand, he longs to return to his barely remembered home and be reunited with his true family in Salem. But he has also found happiness in his life with Bin Aqeel, Sayyida Khadija, and his newfound love, Salma.

Nicola, recognizing the young man's conflicted thoughts, suggests he go to bed and consider it again in the morning.

Of course, Abdullah can't sleep with these thoughts warring in his mind. He doesn't want to regret wasting such a precious opportunity, but he doesn't want to leave without a proper goodbye to Al-Sayyid Bin Aqeel and the foster mother who had so generously cared for him.

Early the next morning, Captain Nicola pays a visit to the office of the American Agency to inform Captain Beckman that the boy they had come looking for is indeed on the ship and has grown into an adolescent, but he is a little perturbed and uncertain whether to return to his country or not. Nicola says he can arrange his escape to join them, but it must be quick, because their ship is departing that evening. He will have to bring Abdullah to them before the sun goes down.

Nicola returns to the ship mid-morning to find Bin Aqeel has issued orders to mobilize and leave Mokha immediately, ruining Nicola's plan.

Time passes heavily on Abdullah's heart as he sits at the bow of the ship heading for Luhayya, giving his back to the missed opportunity. Did he do the right thing, leaving the matter up to Captain Nicola, or should he have taken it in his own hands? Could a person regret what he has not done, more than what he has done?

Captain Nicola approaches him with a mug of coffee in hand, noticing the distant look on Abdullah's face.

"How do you recognize the sound of opportunity when it knocks on your door?" he asks, startling Abdullah with his question.

"I don't know. ... Maybe by listening to your heartbeats. If they are louder than the sound of the knock, maybe you should embrace it? ... But what if opportunity does not knock on your door again?" Abdullah is thinking now about the future.

"Create a door for it, then," Nicola responds.

Abdullah feels as if a new chapter has opened in the book of his future on this earth. But doubts and obsessions leave him struggling to choose between two worlds.

The *Falak* arrives at the entrance to Luhayya, gliding carefully through the coral reef, and heads east to cast its anchor in the harbor. Abdullah is reminded of when he arrived here for the first time with the crew of the *Essex*. He remembers the place well, from the moment they entered mangrove forests circling the archipelago like a green bracelet, further girdled by the shoreline that embarced so many varieties of fish and crustaceans, dropping their eggs to flourish in this richly diverse ecosystem. White seagulls soar overhead, calling in the cloudless sky as if welcoming the visitors.

The *Falak* gently approaches, its hull gliding across tangled thickets of sea plants, to arrive at the ancient dock. Abdullah recognizes the Al-Zayla'i Mosque from a distance, its three rooftop domes rising well above the ancient houses. As the vessel nears the shore, the exquisite patterns adorning the whitewashed Tihami houses begin to reflect the glow of a late afternoon sun. Abdullah contemplates the deeply tanned faces of workers in the port. Salim, the friend he had made here, comes to mind. Could he still be living in his house overlooking the beach? He would so love to meet with him and talk in his language, in which he is now fluent.

As soon as the *Falak* drops anchor, Abdullah asks his father's permission to disembark and takes off running as soon as his feet hit the sand, headed for the north end of the harbor to seek out Salim. Small fishing boats are scattered in the shallow waters to his left as he walks barefoot along the beach. Here he once pursued his favorite pastime of swimming in the afternoon and diving from the ship into the warm water. *It would have been icy cold in the North Atlantic during those same months,* he muses. Facing the coastline from the ship, he would watch camels munching on the leaves of the flowering Avicennia mangroves. He remembers the time of the *azan,* the call to prayer, as the sun sinks below the horizon. When they heard the melodious sound, he and Captain Joseph would drop what they were doing and stand at the bow of the ship to listen to the muezzin's voice.

He recalls wandering through the city's marketplace with Chef Leon, the man from Africa who had been kidnapped right out of his mother's hands and shipped off to the American continent like livestock, then ended up aboard the *Essex* and sailing to his ultimate demise in Yemen. Who knows the reality of that cook's mother and the siblings he left behind, Abdullah wonders. He was a son and brother, possibly an uncle to a new generation who will never know anything about him besides the fact that he left and never returned. *Could my fate be like Leon's?* he wonders.

Half a mile from the dock, the long-awaited meeting takes place between Bin Aqeel and his old ally Al-Sharif Hamoud, at the latter's residence in Qafl Fortress. The initial encounter is cautious, while each party sizes up the other. Bin Aqeel is especially apprehensive. An acknowledgment of reciprocal blame is enough to clear the air. But experience has taught both of them to leave some space between them, such that neither will ever fully depend on the other and make withdrawal impossible.

Contrary to the adults, there is no space for retreat between Abdullah and Salim from the friendship that had brought them together. It has never even occurred to them that they needed to have such a space.

Abdullah finds his friend, who is about two years older, and they enjoy reminiscing about their times together years ago. Now able to speak more easily with Salim, Abdullah relates the news of their ship, the *Essex*, what happened to him and its crew, and how he ended up alone. He tells him of how Bin Aqeel adopted him and took him to Muscat, then to live in Mirbat, and his recent voyage to Basrah. He also tells him about the American ship in Mokha.

He learns from Salim that he has two older brothers: one who joined the army of Al-Mansour Ali, the imam of Yemen in Sana'a, and another who stayed nearby to work for Al-Sharif Hamoud, who has joined the independent tribal rule of the Al-Mikhlaf Al-Sulaymani in Abu Arish after disputes within his family of Aal Khayrat were resolved following his father's death.

Abdullah is not surprised to learn of two brothers working for separate parties, enemies to each other. The political arena is always full of contradictions, as Salim points out. In fact, Al-Sharif Hamoud's hold on his position is thanks to his skill in maintaining a balance between parties whose interests are inconsistent, sometimes conflicting and sometimes agreeing.

Al-Sharif is known for his shrewdness and wisdom in managing the affairs of his emirate, but what most distinguishes his rule is his simultaneous push-and-pull political strategy with various forces.

The two teenagers stroll barefoot along the sandy beach. Abdullah walks a little ahead, prompting Salim to ask him to not walk in front of him, as he might not follow. Then he slows down and lags behind Salim, to which Salim says not to walk behind him, as he might not lead. Salim completes the lesson by asking him to walk by his side so he can be his friend. The two sit together on a weather-worn log facing the sea.

"What are you going to do, now that you let the American ship depart without you?" Salim probes.

"I will do what I've been doing. I'll move from one place to the next with Bin Aqeel, who has taken me in as one of his family," Abdullah responds.

"But ... but what about your other family over there ... there in America?"

A glint of tears suddenly appears in Abdullah's eyes, as if Salim's queries have stirred up the deep sorrow he has been fighting so hard to suppress.

"What about them?" Abdullah asks feebly, trying to sound indifferent and hoping his friend changes the subject.

Salim points to the east and says, "Listen, Abdullah. My older brother works there, for Imam Al-Mansour in Sana'a. He stays there for weeks, sometimes months. I may not understand everything my mother says, but I can always read the longing in her eyes when she says a prayer for my brother when he is gone. Don't you long for them? Aren't you homesick?"

Abdullah gazes at the sun as it dips into the sea, signaling the end of the day.

"I've buried my longing in these waters, just as the sea swallows up the sun."

"And what of your family and your mother? Don't you see you've also buried her longing for you in the waters of the Atlantic, as you have buried yours here?"

Abdullah drops his face into his palms, wincing at the pain of a wound in his chest reopening.

"Still," Salim continues, "the sun returns every day, shining brightly once again. Your longing will rise up again too, even if you're in a different place. I have no doubt about that."

Bin Aqeel unloads the weapons and ammunition he brought onto the wharf for Al-Sharif's men to transfer them to his fort in Qafl. As for the French cannons hidden in the bilges of the *Falak*, horse-drawn wagons may be needed to transport them to the sites Al-Sharif Hamoud has selected. Captain Nicola will set them up and train Al-Sharif's men how to operate them.

That evening, Al-Sharif Hamoud hosts Bin Aqeel for dinner, along with his son Abdullah and Captain Nicola. Abdullah remembers climbing the stairs of the fort when he first came here with Captain Joseph Orne and meeting with Al-Sharif Hamoud in their search for coffee. Once everyone has finished dinner, most of the guests depart, leaving Bin Aqeel and his son with a few of Al-Sharif Hamoud's men and guards standing at the doorway. Cups of locally grown coffee are served.

Al-Sharif leans to speak quietly into Bin Aqeel's ear as he glances toward Abdullah from the corner of his eye.

"So, this is the boy you told me about. He has grown up since the last time I saw him."

"That's him, may God preserve you."

"Do you know that the English sent me a letter asking about him by name? John Paul, if I'm not mistaken."

"And how would I know? And why would they be concerned with a boy that's not even among their countrymen?" Bin Aqeel mutters, talking to himself.

"Let me tell you something else," Al-Sharif continues. "I received a letter from Captain Redland, the British administrator in Mokha, requesting me to arrest you and turn you over to them."

Bin Aqeel fidgets in his seat as he hears these words coming from his host.

"Did you know that the Americans have appointed a commercial agent in Mokha? He is demanding thirty thousand dollars in compensation for the value of their ship, the *Essex*, that you and your men burned. Captain Redland warned me about welcoming the *Falak* because, he claims, the money you used to purchase it was stolen, and that I must arrest you and fine you one hundred thousand dollars."

Nasty suspicions swirl in Bin Aqeel's head. Could Al-Sharif's invitation have been an orchestrated plot by the English to catch him by luring him to Luhayya after they failed to pursue him in the sea? Could Al-Sharif have made a deal with the English to turn him over to them? And why not, since he had yielded to their envoy Pringle before?

A heavy silence comes over the gathering before Bin Aqeel ventures to speak, his eyes fixed on the doorway where Al-Sharif's guards stand, arms in hand.

"And what was your reply, may God preserve you?"

"Can you imagine the audacity of that Christian to order me around? I am the ruler of Al-Mikhlaf Al-Sulaymani! I told him that this matter is private between us and the son of our brother, and you have no right to interfere with cousins, especially because he did not ask you to do so. As for the ship, he procured it with his own money from Al-Sayyid Saeed bin Sultan, the ruler of Oman, which you could verify for yourself. And about arresting you? Oh, how presumptuous of him!

Who does he think he is? I told him that whoever enters in our land, we will decide what to do with him, not someone like you, Redland, telling us how to manage our own property."

Bin Aqeel gulps a deep sigh of relief upon hearing these words from Al-Sharif, as if cold water has just been just poured on him.

The guests finish sipping their coffee and listening to the stories of Al-Sharif Hamoud's ancestors who came from Makkah about two generations before, when their great grandfather, Khayrat bin Shabir bin Abi Nami, emigrated to these southern parts of the peninsula. Abdullah listens intently. He is passionate about the stories of the Arabs, their history, and the tribal battles and wars that took place in the heart of Arabia and at its perimeters.

Al-Sharif reccollects his first war, eight years before, in which his small army was quashed by the battalions sent by Abdulaziz bin Saud, led by his deputy in Asir. These regiments were mobilized from various tribes, including Qahtan, Aal Marra, Al-Dawasir, and Sirat Ubaydah, as well as the tribe of Asir. He spoke of what happened when he met them, and how he insisted, after having seen the killing and looting that the ruler of Najd ordered in Dhamad and its surrounding villages, that he must conclude a peace treaty to bring him under the hegemony of Ibn Saud. This would avoid more bloodshed, providing the treaty was between himself and the ruler of Diriyah, with no middleman.

Al-Sharif finishes his story by telling of his most recent battle, a year ago, against his rival Abu Nuqta, in which the latter met his demise, and all the related events and stories, including getting assistance from the tribe of Banu Yam. The coffee stops circulating among the guests and Bin Aqeel, citing the late hour, takes leave from the gathering. Abdullah is reluctant to go, wishing the night could continue so he might hear more about the Arabs and their stories.

Suddenly, his mind flashes back, hearing his mother's soft voice in Salem as she tells him a bedtime story. The youth leaves with his father in the dark, while the voice of his mother in Salem lingers in his head.

LOST SON OF SALEM: AN AMERICAN BOY'S ODYSSEY IN THE ARAB WORLD

The following morning, Bin Aqeel presents the gifts he brought for Al-Sharif Hamoud: two purebred Arabian steeds, the best of his herd in Mirbat. They have been carried in the hold of the *Falak,* along with costly armor and expensive perfumes. He adds to these the gifts he had intended for the Sultan of Lahj, grateful again for Al-Sharif's stance when the English demanded he arrest him.

Al-Sharif Hamoud accepts the gifts gratefully, and then the two meet privately so Al-Sharif can explain why he had requested the weapons. He tells Bin Aqeel he will need them in the wars he expects to wage on a number of fronts, to expand his emirate against some powerful parties. Under the cover of spreading Wahhabism, his brigades have reached Zabid, then Mokha and its surrounding villages. They also invaded Hudaydah and Bayt al-Faqih and made their way as far as Bab al-Mandab in the south. His competition with Abdulwahhab Abu Nuqta, Ibn Saud's deputy in Asir, has ended with the latter's death. Bin Aqeel realizes that exploiting a fundamentalist school of religious thought was fuel for the campaigns carried out by Ibn Saud and those under his banner, but he knows Al-Sharif Hamoud is too smart to get distracted by pursuits such as preventing people from smoking tobacco, or demolishing their shrines, or chasing after people delinquent in their prayers. Furthermore, Al-Sharif Hamoud personally follows the Shafi'i school of thought, so his embrace of the mission of the shaykhs of Diriyah is merely a ploy to mobilize funds to expand his emirate southwards and ultimately secede altogether from the authority of Ibn Saud.

Al-Sharif Hamoud proposes to Bin Aqeel that he join him in his dream project, namely to broaden his power over a wide swath of the coastal Tihama region, especially since Bin Aqeel has the wealth and experience to play an influential role in recruiting soldiers and supplying the forces with arms, particularly on the sea.

Bin Aqeel listens with extreme interest. He has been hoping to revive his sea adventures, propelled by his political aspirations, after a long lull in which he was preoccupied with commercial activities. Bin Aqeel agrees to participate in Al-Sharif's military operations by providing supply, armament, and recruitment support services, on the condition that he grants him Hudaydah. Al-Sharif does not accept this, because Hudaydah is too valuable a spoil to hand it over easily to Bin Aqeel. The two men agree to a compromise, which is for Al-Sharif Hamoud to appoint Bin Aqeel to preside as emir over the region of Qunfudhah in the Asir province as compensation for his services, providing he promises to carry out this task.

Bin Aqeel recalls the past agreement they made for Kamaran and how the English were able to persuade his friend to change his conditions, so he makes up his mind to request that Al-Sharif guarantee their agreement in writing, irrevocable and immutable.

Bin Aqeel remains in Luhayya for a few weeks while Nicola trains Al-Sharif's men how to use the French cannons they brought with them. Abdullah, spending time with his buddy Salim, tells him of the dreams that have disturbed his sleep since he arrived in Luhayya. Seeing these places that he visited the first time with the crew of the *Essex* has stirred up a multitude of emotions about his family. One dream repeats itself almost every night, in which he sees his mother coming out of the chimney of their house in Salem to fly into the sky and disappear in the clouds above the Atlantic.

"Do you know, Salim, what I fear most?" Abdullah asks, with his face turned to the sky. "That I might forget how she looks, that I cannot remember any of her facial features."

"Is that possible?" Salim asks.

"I don't know, but what about you? What do you fear most?"

Salim ponders briefly before answering the question as he watches Al-Sharif's guards pacing the docks.

"I fear that the confrontations between Al-Sharif Hamoud and the Imam of Yemen will lead my two brothers to battle against each other, and a stray bullet from one of their muskets will kill the other."

Bin Aqeel and Abdullah depart the port of Luhayya and sail for Qunfudhah, about two hundred and fifty miles to the north. This is a reconnaissance trip to inspect what the father hopes will be his new property and the seat of his emirate. The region lies along the ancient caravan route that links Yemen with the Levant, and the town was originally established as a rest stop for caravans where this route meets the streams of Wadi Qanuna, one of the valleys of Sarat. The outpost later expanded, similar to others along the trade route.

Bin Aqeel has barely finished his mission in Qunfudhah when he receives instructions from Al-Sharif to meet him urgently in Hudaydah and to bring with him more supplies, weapons, and ammunition. Bin Aqeel discusses the matter with his son and decides to send Abdullah to Dhofar, bearing messages to the people of Al-Shihr to recruit some men and procure weapons, while he goes to Mokha to search for European mercenaries who are experts on the battlefield and can deploy the cannons that Al-Sharif has taken as booty.

Abdullah's mission is successful, and he brings the *Falak* back, bearing more men and weapons, to meet up with his father in Hudaydah. The two join Al-Sharif Hamoud's battalion, which is fighting on two fronts, one against Al-Mutawakkil, the Imam of Yemen, and one against Ibn Saud's troops.

It has always been Al-Sharif's policy to not launch an attack until he is sure his enemy is busy with a power greater than his, and if he feels overpowered, he does not seek to fight to the bitter end. Rather, he accepts a retreat and withdrawal, or even a temporary alliance, with a power greater than his.

He is not merely a man of war but also a politician. He believes the path to victory lies in endurance, not in numbers, and that authority comes with capability, not with abundance. Luhayya falls to the hands of Ibn Saud's forces for a short time before they withdraw, when Al-Sharif returns from Hudaydah for the two forces to face each other in Abu Arish. Al-Sharif manages to banish Ibn Saud's alliance from his land, but he does not concern himself with pursuing those forces beyond it. He still has a date to keep with the forces of the Imam of Yemen, who are poised to descend from the mountains to Hudaydah.

Bin Aqeel fights with his men side-by-side with Al-Sharif, who has appointed him over a brigade. He proves to have a superior capacity for managing a ground battle, just as he has become known for his expertise as a buccaneer at sea. During the fighting, Abdullah attempts to approach on his horse to join his father, but Bin Aqeel orders him to stay behind with a rearguard of about twenty men, to protect the army's supplies from looting and pillaging. Abdullah turns around, his rifle in hand, while the whir of flying bullets shocks his ears.

He fears the exposed ammunition might explode and asks some of the soldiers to help him carry the boxes to a crevice in the ground, where it will be safer. While the rearguard soldiers are busy moving the boxes, they do not notice a band of about forty men sneaking between their tents, ambushing two men who had stayed behind at the posts and finishing them off. Having benefited from the element of surprise, the infiltrators now make themselves known. Abdullah is the first to fall victim to one of the attackers' bullets, which lodges in his thigh. An unequal battle ensues that soon deteriorates into hands-on combat with cold steel—daggers and swords.

Abdullah bandages his thigh with a strip he tears from his turban and fights with his men to survive, with all the strength he can muster. Casualties fall on both sides: eight of Al-Sharif's men and fifteen from the attackers. Abdullah retreats from the confrontation, dragging his leg, while his remaining men try to reload their rifles with gunpowder, possibly for the last time. They know that their attackers will not give up until they finish them off and steal the store of ammunition.

Abdullah and a small company of men retreat behind a dirt mound to hide from enemy fire. His life flashes before his eyes, as he remembers the Derby Wharf and his friend Henry, playing together in the port of Salem. An image of his father working in the stable appears before him, then his mother calling him to wash his hands before going up to his room. He feels the sway of the *Essex* in the midst of the storm in the Atlantic …

He snaps out of his delirium with a poke from his companion, who is pointing at the blood flowing from his leg, warning him to tighten the bandage. Will this place become his grave, thousands of miles from his birthplace? No, not yet. He jumps up, recalling the words of Al-Sharif: *Victory lies in endurance, not in numbers … with capability, not abundance.*

Abdullah looks his friend in the eyes, sees his eyebrows full of dust from the blowing sand, and recognizes in those eyes the wild-eyed fear that is also deep inside him. That zap of fear is sharper than a dagger or sword. Fear blocks us from thinking straight, Abdullah knows. He realizes he must set his fear aside and must decide something, anything. Nothing gives the fearful one courage more than knowing that his enemy is also fearful.

An idea comes to his mind. He orders his men to point their rifles at one of the open boxes of gunpowder some distance below them on the hill. Then he props himself up with a hand on his companion's shoulder and shouts in the deepest voice he can muster—loud enough for the enemy to hear—that reinforcements are their way, he can see them now, with only their horses' heads blocking the view. Shots are fired, piercing the box of gunpowder, and Abdullah falls to the ground, drenched in blood.

Ibn Saud's alliance is defeated. Al-Sharif's forces have prevailed and are able to maintain control of their territory.

Then comes the bitterest phase of the battle: of burying the dead, treating the injured, exchanging prisoners, and reuniting.

Abdullah forces his eyes open and finds himself in a tent, his father and a few servants at his side. Al-Sharif Hamoud stops briefly near him, then moves on to the other injured soldiers. He is calling, "Salim, Salim!" Abdullah thinks at first that he is asking for his friend Salim but then realizes he is saying the word itself, reassuring the injured that they made it out safe and secure.

He tries to shift position, and an intense pain shoots through his thigh, almost knocking him unconscious. He notices the agonized moans of the wound and the stench of death that permeates this place. Abdullah looks at the shrouded corpse next to him and tries to determine who he might be.

He learns it is none other than the youth who had stayed with him to the last moments, asking him whether death is painful. Abdullah had not answered, because he didn't know, nor did he think anyone else knew the answer. But now he considers that perhaps life is more painful than death. Some victories are worse than defeat.

Once Bin Aqeel is reassured that his son will recover, he tells him that his tactic succeeded in sparing the lives of the rest of the rearguard men. When the gunpowder box exploded, the attackers thought a brigade of Al-Sharif's men was on its way to save them, and they turned on their heels in fright, leaving the ammunition untouched.

Abdullah remains in the tent, being treated with the other wounded men for a few days. The healer extracts the metal from his thigh, which fortunately only penetrated his muscle and did not reach the bone. He is then moved to Al-Sharif's administrative seat, prepared for Bin Aqeel and his assistants on the west side of Abu Arish.

Abdullah recovers from his wound and stays with his father, who remains loyal to Al-Sharif, providing his army with supplies, supporting him when needed, and expressing his opinion and advice in managing Al-Sharif's military operations. His expertise in rapid travel by sea and maritime routes and his relationship with French mercenaries able to operate and maintain cannons make him a valuable asset for his ally.

Chapter Seven

In the summer of 1810, on the other side of the world, a young port worker in Salem watches a ship raise a flag indicating that it belongs to Mr. Orne. He watches it slowly pass among dozens of other ships through the mouth of the harbor and drop anchor at Derby Wharf. He is curious about where exactly the ship has been, because he knows someone who may be aboard. An hour past noon, sailors begin to unload the cargo, which he can tell from the scents wafting past his nose includes all sorts of spices and coffee. The youth's curiosity grows as he approaches the ship and asks questions of one of the disembarking sailors, who tells him they are just arrived from a long voyage to Yemen and that the captain of the ship is Captain Beckman.

Soon after, the captain himself sets foot on the wharf, carrying the ship's record under his arm, while the youth's eyes follow him. The captain speaks with his first mate, then leaves the wharf once he is reassured that the cargo is in trusted hands. The youth follows close behind, making every effort to not lose sight of him, until he reaches the Orne company's office.

The youth sneaks around the back to try to eavesdrop from an open window. He hears the captain and William Orne, the ship's owner, exchange greetings. Orne congratulates Beckman on his safe return, then invites him to sit down for a cup of coffee.

"Thank God for His protection. Our ships coming from the Arabian Peninsula have a special status with me."

"How is that?" Beckman asks.

"Our trade there is flourishing and our goods from Yemen have afforded us great profits, despite of the sorrows we faced in the beginning."

"I am pleased to be a part of your success, but—"

"How is the trade office we set up in Mokha doing? Were its services good?" Orne asks.

"Before we talk business, Mr. Orne, there is something I would like to ask you about."

"Of course, go ahead."

"I know that you might not like this subject, but I must verify it."

"Verify what? What matter do you mean?"

"It has to do with your devastated ship, the *Essex*."

Orne puts down his coffee, all ears now.

"I don't want to open old wounds, and I know that your nephew was one of the victims, but do you remember if there was a young boy on that ship?"

Orne coughs out the smoke from his cigar as he peers into Beckman's eyes.

"What? Yes, yes, Herman Paul's son was part of the crew. I remember when he brought his son here, to this office, to ask for permission for him to travel. We sat here and discussed it. Terrible thing, to lose one so young. But why do you ask?"

"Are you sure, Mr. Orne, of what you say, that the boy is John, the son of Herman Paul?"

"Yes, I could double-check in the ship's record kept here, but once again, why do you ask?"

"John Herman Paul is alive. The news you received that all members of the *Essex* crew had perished was not accurate."

The young man listening outside the window, named Henry, jumps up in shock and runs like the wind, dodging the goods heaped up everywhere around the port, taking the same route he used to take when playing with his friend John when they were little. He stops to catch his breath in front of a large square house, the place where they used to part ways, Henry returning home while John continued on farther. Henry runs again, this time until he reaches John's home, where he spots Herman Paul standing at his doorstep. Henry shouts from a distance, still running.

"Mr. Paul! ... Mr. Paul!"

Herman has partially lost his hearing since he fell from the roof of a barn he was building a couple of years ago.

"John ... John ..." Henry cries out, panting, as he arrives at the house.

Herman Paul knows Henry well. He was his son's best friend. He is not surprised to see him, but he wonders why he is running in such a panic.

"John ... John is alive!" Henry blurts, trying to catch his breath.

"Who?" Herman tries to think of all the Johns he knows, all except his son.

"Your son John ... is alive and well," Henry pants. "I was at Mr. Orne's office and I overheard one of his ship captains say that John did not die on the *Essex* disaster."

This idea has just started to sink into the man's mind when the two hear a thump behind the door. Herman rushes inside to find that his wife, apparently having heard Henry's shouts, has fainted on the floor. The two pick her up and lay her on the sofa swing on the front porch. Some minutes later, Faith opens her eyes to find William Orne and Captain Beckman standing on the porch, talking with her husband. Orne notices that Faith has begun to stir and nods to the others.

"Is it true what I heard?" she says, trembling.

"Hello, Mrs. Paul. This is—" But before Orne can finish, she repeats the question.

"Is it true what I heard?"

"What did you hear?" Orne asks, cautiously.

"My son John is still alive?"

"Yes, this news is true and has been confirmed by Captain Beckman." Orne smiles as he indicates the man standing next to him.

"Did you see him with your own two eyes?" she asks Beckman. "Come closer, let me see the eyes that saw into my son's eyes."

Uneasily, the captain draws closer and leans over for her to look in his eyes, but she recoils and says, "You did not see him. Something in your eyes tells me you did not see him!"

"Yes, that is correct," Beckman responds, taken aback, and astonished like the others.

"What? But I thought you said that—" Orne asks angrily.

"I did not say that I saw him myself, but I did see the person who saw him ... with my own two eyes," he tells Orne.

Beckman proceeds to relate his story about the Arab woman in Mokha who told them about John in the trade office, and about his meeting with the Frenchman, Captain Nicola, who confirmed that John was aboard the ship. He had not merely met him but had tried to arrange his escape to the American ship, but alas, this was not to be. The "pirate" ship that he was working on left abruptly.

"Please believe me, dear lady," he says gently. "I swear by the Almighty that all I have said is true and that your son John is alive."

Faith lets out a deep sigh as she hears her son's name spoken by a person recently come away from the land to which she had entrusted her son.

"I believe you, I believe you. It's enough to know that you laid your eyes on the one who saw him. You are living proof that, as terrible a disappointment as it is for him not to be home, there is yet hope, praise our Lord in Heaven." The best she could have hoped for, for many long years now, was to someday visit John's grave, but now she has renewed hope that he will be the one paying a visit. She tilts her head towards her husband and whispers, "Allow hope, not pain, to forge our future."

With the arrival of fall, Bin Aqeel receives a letter from someone he knows in Mauritius who informs him that the French government, represented by General Decaen, has executed a judicial order to seize what remains of his properties there. Bin Aqeel is aware that a few years earlier, the French governor had issued a warrant for his arrest in the death of Chapelain, over which the hapless Captain Denault had been jailed for his inability to prevent it. But he has not been aware until this moment that his properties have been seized. Bin Aqeel considers his valuable assets on the island, especially the sugar plantations near Port Louis that he had worked hard to reclaim. He had intended to return and benefit from those assets but now realizes they have vanished from his grip.

He decides to write to Napoleon Bonaparte, emperor of France, who is busy waging wars in Europe now. The letter bemoans his maltreatment by the deputy in Mauritius and reflects on his long history of providing services to the French in that region of the Arabian Sea. Bin Aqeel describes how his friendship with the French has cost him dearly and led to his being hunted by the English to the point that he is restricted in his movement, unable to go to India to pursue his trade there. All this has caused him great harm, and here he is now, flabbergasted to find out that his assets have been seized, and by whom? By his allies, the French!

Bin Aqeel is just about to send his letter to Napoleon when the news comes that Mauritius, long a French possession, has fallen to the hands of the English, signaling the end of an era of French control over that section of the southern Arabian Sea and adjacent part of the Red Sea. The new stars of the scene are indubitably the English, who are fast cementing their presence in these waters.

Bin Aqeel is overwhelmed with regret; with this shift of power in the region, it will be very difficult to recover his properties. With the English prevailing over land and sea, the future has become much more uncertain. So Bin Aqeel continues to serve under Al-Sharif's forces, ensuring their resources, for more than a year. He and Abdullah spend this time moving within the Al-Mikhlaf Al-Sulaimani emirate.

Wherever Al-Sharif's campaigns lead them, they go, and wherever they stop, they stay.

Bin Aqeel has no time to focus on Qunfudha because Al-Sharif's theater of operations is mostly in the south, but occasionally he finds time to visit his brother Abdulrahman in Mokha, who has become a safe conduit for communication, forwarding messages to and from his wife, who is "holding the fort" in Mirbat. He sends letters through his brother to his connections in Mauritius, Muscat, Bombay, and the Malabar Coast to seek out their news, especially of any British movements that might limit his freedom.

Among the letters he delivers by way of his brother is to Oman, asking one of his agents about the ship he has ordered to be built there.

In early 1812, Al-Sharif Hamoud's military operations come to a halt when he signs a peace treaty with Ibn Saud, and the Imam of Yemen stops launching raids on the southern ports of Tihama. Bin Aqeel feels that his role in the land of Mikhlaf is coming to a close and that the services he has been providing to Al-Sharif's army are no longer crucial. So he asks his friend's permission to return home to Dhofar.

Al-Sharif reminds him of his promise to hand him Qunfudha, but Bin Aqeel chooses to return home while expressing appreciation for Al-Sharif's fealty to him. He longs to work freely, and his stay in Qunfudha would keep him under the umbrella of Al-Sharif's rule, while his homeland in Dhofar awaits him with no competition from anyone.

He departs with his son and men after bidding farewell to Al-Sharif Hamoud, riding on the camels Al-Sharif had provided as a farewell gift, laden with provisions and gifts in appreciation of Bin Aqeel's distinguished service. They head south to Luhayya, where they stop for a day. The convoy sets up camp on the edge of town, allowing their mounts to settle and rest. Abdullah seizes this as a perfect opportunity to visit his friend Salim.

LOST SON OF SALEM: AN AMERICAN BOY'S ODYSSEY IN THE ARAB WORLD

Darkness falls as Abdullah reaches Salim's home. It differs little from the other little huts in this area, built on stone foundations, and Abdullah is lost for a moment. The huts are scattered along the coastline and look so much alike. They all have high, conical ceilings made of twisted reeds fastened with ropes and wood planks. He nears one from which a thin column of smoke is rising and a soft light is glowing inside.

Could this be Salim's house? It seems to pulsate with life, revealing the soul of its inhabitants. *Life begins in the home,* he thinks. *It is also where it ends, for many people.* Abdullah stands in the dark contemplating this modest hut, stirring up memories of his small home in Salem. *A home is made by who is in it, not by the walls around it.* That is what his mother used to say, but now he realizes her image is fading from his memory. He wrings his memories hard to keep her features in his mind's eye. The place worth calling *home* is the place that will miss you when you leave, he hypothesizes.

The sound of Salim gleefully calling out to him interrupts his contemplative thoughts. The two happily greet each other after Abdullah's two-year absence. Abdullah sees the joy in his friend's face as he tells him that his two brothers have both returned home, after serving in opposing armies, fighting each other. The small family has been reunited. Abdullah greets Salim's mother and congratulates her on the comforting return of her two sons. She responds with a prayer that he may be reunited with his loved ones and insists he stay for dinner.

They all sit around the meal, which consists of millet bread, boiled sorghum kernels, and some fruit and milk. Salim tells his mother how Abdullah was separated from his family as a young boy and how his past sometimes comes back to haunt him. Looking down at her food, she says to him, "Your memories, my son, are like salt. The right amount gives food a good flavor, but too much ruins it. If you always live in your past, you will not have a present to remember in the future." Abdullah asks her how a mother can endure missing her children, to which she answers, "Did you see the grasses in the pasture on your way here?"

"Yes", he replies.

"And did you see the cattle grazing?"

"Yes."

"It is only through patience, my son, that those grasses turn into the milk that we drink."

Abdullah bids the family goodbye, ducking his head through the low doorway of the hut as he leaves. Salim insists that he spend the night with them, but Abdullah declines and asks Salim to accompany him to the edge of the village, where their camp is set up, so he doesn't get lost. He would always prefer to walk in the dark with his friend than to walk alone in the sunlight. Abdullah asks his friend what his mother's secret is to maintaining her enviably good health; there is a glow in her face that is lacking in his own, though he is half her age. Salim tells him there is no secret, besides her refusal to hold malice towards anyone. As she always says to her sons, someone who holds a grudge is like the man who drinks poison and waits for someone else to die from it. As they walk along, Salim asks if he is still having that recurring dream.

"No," Abdullah tells him.

"Do you remember our conversation, the last time we met, about our worst fears?"

"Yes."

"I thank God that my worst fears did not come true. Even though my brothers were soldiers in two competing armies, pointing their guns at each other, God protected them for their mother's sake, and they returned safe and sound. Neither had to shoot a bullet to kill his brother. Do you know that we are planning to leave this place?"

"But to where?"

"We will go to Al-Zahraa, a new town planned by Al-Sharif Hamoud in Wadi Moor. I heard that Al-Sharif dug wells and built a great fortress there, and will offer funds to whoever establishes homes and farms. We'll work there, I and my brothers, instead of the life we have here."

Abdullah wishes him the best in his new life with his brothers and mother in Al-Zahraa.

"But what about you?" Salim asks.

"What about me?"

"You haven't told me about your worst fears!"

Abdullah stops for a moment, trying to remember.

"I fear, my friend, that the day will come when you will not be able to picture her in your mind's eye."

The camel caravan resumes its journey in the early morning, heading south for Hudayda by way of the plains of Tihama and through Al-Sharif Hamoud's territory, passing Al-Sirat to their left and the sea to their right. The caravan goes by Hudayda without stopping and continues on through Wadi Rimaa, verdant with fields of sorghum, millet, and bananas. A herd of camels saunters in front of the caravan, prompted by the camel driver's melodic chanting. The valley exudes the fragrance of *kadhi*, the spiky screw palm flowers. Bin Aqeel prods his camel into a new direction, and the caravan turns with him slightly left toward the east and the town of Zabid, where they will stop for the night and replenish their water supply from the ancient well next to the Al-Asha'ira Mosque. The town lies about halfway down the coastal plains, between the sea and the mountains, and is home to a small garrison established by Al-Sharif. There are scattered ruins that appear to have once been ancient classrooms, revealing the people's long history of pursuing knowledge.

Here, Bin Aqeel visits an old woman, a relative he has not seen for a long time, while the rest of the travelers settle down to sleep after the long day on camelback.

Abdullah had hoped to explore the town, which he had not visited before, but the weariness of travel makes him wake up too late. The sun has already risen above the horizon and the convoy is packed and ready to go. Bin Aqeel's caravan departs, headed for its last stop within Al-Sharif's territory southwards to Mokha, passing through Wadi Zabid, a place for which the Prophet of Islam had once prayed a blessing.

The small caravan arrives at a beach a few miles north of Mokha, then continues its trip to arrive at the city mid-morning. Bin Aqeel spends the rest of the day with his brother Abdulrahman, after a brief stop to pray at the Shadhili Mosque, as is his custom whenever he visits this town.

The rest of the travelers set up camp on the edge of town. His brother informs him as soon as he arrives that the large *baghla* ship he had commissioned his agent in Sur to build has docked in Mokha and is awaiting instructions. Bin Aqeel sends one of his men back to the camp to call on Abdullah to supervise the transport of their cargo on the camels to their new ship.

There has been a great increase in trade in Mokha, Abdulrahman tells him, with an influx of foreign ships, especially since the recent military incursions ended with a truce, which has brought relative stability to the region. With a rise in buying and selling between ports, there is increasing need for cargo vessels, which motivated Abdulrahman to buy the rights to transport the goods of some tradesmen to Dhofar, Muscat, Bombay, and Zanzibar. He suggests to his brother that they use the new *baghla* as part of the fleet he intends to lease.

Bin Aqeel does not object to leasing his ship. At one hundred and forty feet, the vessel can carry three hundred tons of goods. And he will be departing with a mostly empty ship, save some personal supplies and the gifts he has brought with him.

Bin Aqeel spends two nights in Mokha while the ship is loaded with its new cargo. To his brother he has given all the camels that carried his caravan to this last land stop, as well as gifts he brought from

Al-Sharif. He has also entrusted him with money for the woman he has seen begging passersby at the Shadhili Mosque, though he missed seeing her this time.

At mid-morning on the third day, while Bin Aqeel is touring the port to ensure all is ready for their departure, he overhears a conversation. Someone is negotiating with another ship, asking to be taken to Muscat and be allowed to pay later. But the ship's representative refuses, demanding he pay the fare up front.

Bin Aqeel recognizes the man's dialect easily; it is not a Yemeni accent but rather, he presumes, that of someone from Ras al-Khaima or Sharjah, or possibly Khor Fakkan in Al-Shumailia, which Bin Aqeel knows well. The man appears to possess no more than the clothes he is wearing and a slave who accompanies him.

An hour later, Abdullah comes to inform his father that they are ready to embark. He also asks if they could transport to Muscat a man he has just met, and his companion. They have promised to pay for their passage with two of the finest horses from the Qasimi stable.

Bin Aqeel smiles, knowing his son's passion for horses, but how could this travel-weary man own horses at the Qasimi stable, famous for their quality and costliness? Bin Aqeel departs on his new ship, which he has named *Al-Sharifa*, along with his son and the rest of the men, taking with them their memories of the land and leaving only camel tracks in the sand.

The *Sharifa* launches south to Bab al-Mandab. Before it crosses the narrow Iskandar corridor, between the island of Mayyun and the coast of Yemen, Bin Aqeel asks Captain Nicola to lower the sails and stop near one of the rocky outcrops at Ras Minhali. The captain presumes that Bin Aqeel wishes to test the masts of his new vessel, but Bin Aqeel seems to be looking for something ... no, not on the ship, but at the edge of the sea. He looks briefly towards the coast to survey the contours of the land, then turns again to look at the sea, as if trying to fix his sight on something specific. Suddenly, the Sayyid calls for his first mate, a good swimmer, and asks him to dive in at a specific spot to search for his favorite box, one lost two years before, when a sailor accidentally dropped it as they passed through this place. In amazement, everyone on the ship holds their breath, as if they were the one who has just dived into the water. No more than two minutes pass before the sailor resurfaces, sucking in air, box in hand. The wood has decayed somewhat, but the porcelain tea set inside appears to be in pristine condition.

The *Sharifa's* sails are raised again to continue its journey. It turns to port after passing through Bab al-Mandab, then takes a northeastward course, passing by Aden, now under the rule of the Lahj Sultanate, and enters deep into the Arabian Sea, propelled like an arrow by the southwestern winds towards Dhofar.

Abdullah spends most of his time at Captain Nicola's side on deck, as ordered by his father, so that he may gain more experience in navigating and reading maps. He can't help noticing that the man they had agreed to allow to travel with them speaks very little and avoids mixing with the rest of the sailors in their cabins. Even at meal times, he prefers to eat alone once his slave has brought him his share of food. The stranger spends his time on deck watching clouds form in the sky over the sea or gazing at the horizon, as if expecting something.

He gives the impression of being a man of stature who has fallen on hard times, which have tossed him in with these rough sailors. The *Sharifa* now passes by Mukalla, then Shihr, followed by Qishn eastwards along the coast. As it nears Mirbat, Abdullah approaches the man's servant, who speaks Swahili, and tells him that his father Bin Aqeel is from this place. He points to Mirbat, trying to get some word out of the man.

The servant seems hesitant at first to speak about his master, but Abdullah's conversation about his father seems to have broken the ice. Eventually, he reveals that his master is none other than Sultan bin Saqr, shaykh of the Qasimi clan. Previously jailed by Ibn Saud in

Diriyah, he managed to escape the prison. Instead of travelling east towards his homeland in Sharjah, he went west to hide from his pursuers and ended up in Jiddah on the Red Sea coast. But he was not able to leave from there because the city was ruled by Ibn Saud, so he headed surreptitiously south, taking cover by way of Sirat until he reached Mokha, which was under Al-Sharif's control, where he ultimately met the ship's crew.

Abdullah tells his father what he has learned and Bin Aqeel immediately invites the shaykh to stay in his cabin. But the shaykh declines, preferring to spend the rest of the trip in the same place he has chosen among the sailors. But at Bin Aqeel's insistence, he does accept an invitation to dinner, and this time sits at Bin Aqeel's table in the company of Captain Nicola and Abdullah. The young man is all ears, listening intently to the Qasimi shaykh's news about his relations with Rahmah bin Jaber and his escape from the prison of Ibn Saud. The shaykh speaks of the great impact Ibn Saud has had since he established a base for his forces in Al-Buraimi, and how, in spite of the long-standing alliance between Ibn Saud and his Qasimi clan, Ibn Saud ousted him from the tribal shaykhdom and appointed Hussain bin Ali Shaykh Al-Rams in his stead, who pledged to deliver a fifth of the battle spoils that his men seized to Diriyah.

Ibn Saud then returned to capture Shaykh Sultan bin Saqr and send him to his prison in Diriyah after their garrison had invaded the forts of Al-Fujaira, Al-Batina, and Khor Fakkan. It was during those months of 1810 that Ibn Saud's influence reached its height. He tightened his grip from Al-Ahsa in the eastern region of the Arabian peninsula, until his rule spanned from the shores of Kuwait in the north to Al-Buraimi in the south on the edge of Oman, covering Bahrain, Qatar, and Al-Qatif, which he commissioned to his deputy, Bin Ofaisan.

This rule did not last long before it began to diminish, starting with the 1811 campaign of Al-Sayyid Saeed, the sultan of Oman, against Ibn Saud's garrison in Al-Zabara in Qatar and Khor Hassaan, during which he burned and demolished Al-Zabara. Shortly thereafter, Rahmah bin Jaber moved his headquarters from Khor Hassaan to his fort in Dammam, having represented Ibn Saud's naval authority in that region of the Persian Gulf until this time.

The *Sharifa* stops at Masirah Island to replenish its water supply, then sails on towards Ras Al-Hadd, veering to the left to take a northwesterly route to Muscat, a mere hundred and twenty-five miles away. Here, the southwest trade winds die down, calming the waves. This would have made the remainder of the trip to Muscat a little dull, if not for the stories the shaykh relates to Abdullah about the Qasimis and their conflicts with the English.

The *Sharifa* arrives at its destination at a time when the winds are not blowing in the most desirable way. Sultan Saeed's interests have shifted from Bin Aqeel's previous visit to Muscat. The Sultan continues to have a troubled relationship with the ruler of Diriyah, with occasional skirmishes happening along the kingdom's borders, but the Sultan maintains some degree of mutual amicability with the English. One can't fight everyone all at once.

Abdullah thinks about how Al-Sharif Hamoud would handle a variety of adversaries at one time; how he wouldn't change his approach to an enemy unless he learned his rival was preoccupied with something greater than him. How, if he senses he is in a weak position or his opponent has defeated him, he does not pursue the battle and instead retreats and seeks a truce.

The *Sharifa* lowers its anchor in the port to allow the Qasimi shaykh to disembark, concealed by the dark of night. First, though, the shaykh agrees to send the two steeds he had promised to Mirbat as soon as possible.

At the moment, the sultan is occupied with recovering the city of Shinas from the grip of Ibn Saud's forces, after taking back Samail Fort from Mutlaq Al-Mutairi, the commander of Ibn Saud's army. Al-Mutairi has withdrawn to his headquarters in Al-Buraimi, but left behind a garrison forty miles away from Muscat, which poses a direct threat to the sultan.

Despite his careful attempt to escape notice, the Qasimi shaykh is recognized by some spies infiltrating the port area as he leaves the *Sharifa*. This information is passed on to the palace, making the Al-Sultan Saeed disinclined to accept a visit from Bin Aqeel. The Omani sultan's relationship with the Qasimi clan is no better than his relationship with Ibn Saud, so Bin Aqeel makes up his mind to leave Muscat and return to his home in Mirbat, as soon as he has delivered his brother's merchandise to the buyers and received payment. He has seen enough warring and battling in the land of Mikhlaf. He no longer cares to be caught in the middle of these endless crisscrossing disputes among various forces, each claiming its right to leadership. He needs some time to relax with his family and take a rest from the toil of travel.

Abdullah returns to Mirbat with another desire, a longing he has not experienced before, a yearning from the depths of his heart to see Salma, his youthful companion, whom he has not set eyes on for two years.

He returns eager to tell her about his adventures in Mikhlaf, what happened on land and sea, the people he saw, and of his friend Salim, to whom he bade farewell as he was preparing to move with his family to the new city of Al-Zahraa.

Her son's feelings for Salma are not lost on someone with the intuition and wisdom of Sayyida Khadija. She suggests to Bin Aqeel that Abdullah should marry her maidservant Salma. But Bin Aqeel asks her to take it slow, perhaps so they can prepare a suitable time and place for the couple, or possibly to verify Abdullah's desire to do so.

Abdullah does not need to verify his love for Salma, or her love for him. His love for her gives her safety and assurance, and her love for him gives him patience and steadfastness. He is certainly enamored with her.

He does not sleep on the night of his return, imagining a reality that could be better than his dreams. Who says there is a right time and place for love? It just happens by chance, without planning, in a heartbeat, a quiver of an eyelash, or a twinkle of an eye. Love is a refreshing cool breeze wafting over a sailboat floating on a gentle deep blue sea. You can hardly see it as it caresses your cheeks, but you can certainly feel it in your chest and in your breath. He does not know where the sea breeze will take him, but he does want to have his future mapped out before he brings the subject of marriage up with his mother.

Bin Aqeel tightens his control of Dhofar, the land of frankincense and myrrh, leading it with the sharp eye of an expert not lacking in knowledge or good management. Dhofar is the gateway to the sultanate of Muscat on the Indian Ocean and the link between it and the other part of its kingdom on the east coast of Africa. Bin Aqeel maintains the good relations he has had with Al-Sultan Saeed in the past, in spite of the coolness the latter showed him after rumors spread that Bin Aqeel might be involved in supporting the Qasimis. He is still managing to stay out of view of the English. He avoids sea travel now, leaving that to his loyal men, and he has sent Captain Nicola off on the *Saqqoof* bearing merchandise to sell in Southeast Asia.

He has also granted the first mate who had accompanied Abdullah on his voyage to Basrah the freedom to pursue trade using the rest of his ships throughout the Arabian Sea and Zanzibar. This assistant is Yahya, Sayyida Khadija's uncle. Bin Aqeel has often left his wife in the care of this uncle in Mirbat while he was away, and had done so even during the time the father and son spent in the land of Mikhlaf.

In 1814, two years after his return to Mirbat, Bin Aqeel is spending most of his time on land, pinned down by the growing number of British ships plying these waters. He has left sailing to other family members, assistants, and workers, though it's not easy for him to give up life on the sea. Short trips between Mirbat, Taqah, and Salalah don't satisfy his travel hunger, but these are blissful times for Sayyida Khadija. She has been happy to have her small family settled down and feels ready to again bring up the matter of her son's marriage to Salma.

One day, a secret message relayed to her husband from the Bombay governor, Jonathan Duncan, arrives with an envoy of his brother Abdulrahman. In the letter, Duncan states that the British government has chosen to abandon its pursuit of Bin Aqeel after deciding there is no benefit to mobilizing resources for such a mission, considering the many more pressing matters keeping the empire busy in this region.

Once he verifies the authenticity of the letter, Bin Aqeel takes a deep, long breath, gazing toward the sea he has long been forbidden from entering, feeling like a man just released from prison. Days later, he asks Abdullah to prepare for a voyage to Mokha to deliver some goods, including horses, frankincense and myrrh, to Abdulrahman. Abdullah departs on the *Sharifa*, accompanied by Yahya, his first mate and mother's uncle, after bidding farewell to his father and saving his goodbye to Salma to the very last moment, so she would be the last to look into his eyes.

At the moment the *Sharifa* arrives in Mokha, Abdullah spots a ship leaving the port, bearing what appears to be the American flag. His heart races as he sees the ship headed southwards in the opposite direction of their course. He considers turning the ship around and sailing behind it to determine its origin, but Yahya's glare and the thoughts of the mission they came to complete force him to adjust his thinking.

"Maybe it was just a mirage, or a specter from a dream?" he muses aloud, directing his question to Yahya, as if expecting the latter to confirm the thought.

"Stay on the course you chose, Abdullah. You cannot follow every ship you see sailing the opposite of your course."

The *Sharifa* drops anchor in a port teeming with foreign ships. The next morning, its arrival is registered in the ship registry office. It has been a long time since a ship belonging to Bin Aqeel announced its presence in the city where the British magistrate resides. But now the danger of his holdings being pursued is gone.

Abdullah finds this an opportune moment to inquire at the office about the ship he had seen departing the night before and whether it was actually an American ship. To his surprise, it was not just American, but hailed from Salem, his hometown. He could not help but ponder the fact that, if only he had arrived a few hours earlier, he could have sent a letter to his family, to let them know how he was. It is their right, he thinks, after ten years, to at least know that he is alive and well.

Abdullah spends the day with Abdulrahman, going from shop to shop to sell his father's merchandise. He and his uncle visit the Shadhili Mosque, but there is no trace of the woman his father has asked to be given some money. He spends the night in his uncle's home, which has become a forum for the city's traders to gather and exchange news about their city and events farther abroad, brought across the sea by sailors and across the land by caravans to Mokha.

Here Abdullah learns of the death of the ruler of Diriyah, Saud bin Abdulaziz, son of the imam Muhammad bin Saud. He also hears about the military expedition the Egyptians are planning to reconquer parts of the Arabian Peninsula in the name of the Ottomans. So far, Qunfudha has fallen into their hands and now they are on their way to Yemen, having also seized the Holy Sites along the way. This campaign is spearheaded by the new governor of Egypt, Muhammad Ali Pasha, who is waging a war against the ruler of Diriyah on behalf of the Supreme Empire in the Arabian Peninsula, the aim being to reclaim the Hijaz region, which in the hands of Ibn Saud has threatened the Ottomans' religious sovereignty. With his death and the succession of his son Abdullah to power, no one knows exactly what will happen, especially considering how the fortified bases set up in Taif have revealed the growing influence of Egypt on the Arabian Peninsula.

LOST SON OF SALEM: AN AMERICAN BOY'S ODYSSEY IN THE ARAB WORLD

On his way from the port back to his uncle's house just before sundown, Abdullah decides to stop at the tomb of Al-Shadhili. He notices a woman wrapped in a cloak, begging for whatever charity the passersby might provide. He approaches her, thinking she may be the woman his father asked him to help. He knows nothing about her or why Bin Aqeel is concerned with her.

He is barely close enough to ask her name when she suddenly grabs his hand in a steely grip, so that he drops the bag of money his father sent with him into her lap. Startled, Abdullah tries to yank his hand away, but she steals a glimpse at his blue eyes and shrieks, "You are Abdullah! It's you!"

She swiftly conjures up the memory of the young boy as he bathed in the cistern on Kamaran, while the women listened to Sayyida Khadija telling Zainab she intended to adopt him as her own. Abdullah leaves the bag with her and rushes away, reciting some verses of the Qur'an to protect him from what he thinks might be the evil eye.

That night, he tosses and turns, unable to sleep because the old dream has come back to haunt him, the one where he sees his mother rising up out of the chimney of their house in Salem and into the sky, where she disappears into the clouds above the Atlantic Ocean.

Within a week of Abdullah's arrival in Mokha, he has sold most of the goods he brought with him. Whatever is left he decides to leave in the hands of Abdulrahman and return to Mirbat. He feels an irresistible urge, though, before he leaves Mokha, to visit the office of the American Agency licensed to manage coffee company interests. He remembers that he was almost introduced to it four years earlier by way of Captain Nicola. Hesitantly, he enters the small office, not knowing what awaits him inside.

There is a memory that chases him and a dream he suspects won't leave his sleep until he quenches his desire for some news, however small, of his parents and the people in Salem. Do they still remember him when they think back on the people of their city who left their world? Or have they long forgotten him, assuming he died with the others on the *Essex*? The office manager notes his arrival but, assuming he is a local, doesn't raise his gaze from the pile of papers on his desk, which have clearly absorbed his attention for some time. Abdullah introduces himself with a hesitant mix of English and Arabic, enough to catch the attention of the American agent, who speaks Arabic well.

After explaining himself for a few short moments, which feel like an eternity to Abdullah, the astonished agent understands exactly who is standing before him. He looks at Abdullah's blue eyes and the blond wisps dangling from the edge of his turban, which he wears in the style of people from Dhofar. He has no doubt that this young man is the very John Paul he had tried four years ago to smuggle away from Bin Aqeel's ship. He invites him to take a seat, but Abdullah says he prefers to remain standing. The agent informs him that his family in Salem is aware that he is alive and confirms that his parents are alive and well. He says the ship that departed a week before was indeed from Salem and bore a passenger that he might know well.

At this, Abdullah's heart begins to race.

"The ship was carrying your friend Henry. That's what he said to me. Do you know someone by that name?" The world swirls around him as he hears the name Henry for the first time since he arrived in this part of the world.

"Henry ... Henry was here in Mokha?" Abdullah blurts. Suddenly, he feels acutely dizzy; he drops into the nearest chair to keep from falling. It's a strange feeling after being hardened against sea sickness by years of sailing. The rolling of the sea and the roar of pounding waves is nothing compared to the wooziness of the soul and the turbulence of pounding memories.

Once Abdullah recovers his balance and anchors himself on the shore of reality, the office agent brings him a cup of hot coffee. He explains that it is too late to catch up with his friend's ship, not to mention that the season for ships coming from America has ended, but there is still an opportunity for him to return to his homeland. An English cargo ship will be leaving in two months to Liverpool, upon which the American agency officer will be travelling. From there he will cross the Atlantic to New York. Abdullah could travel with him, if he so wishes, of course.

Abdullah listens to the agent, still reeling from the shock of knowing that Henry had come to Yemen on the ship that left the week before. He could have met with his childhood friend, if only he had listened to his own intuition, given in to the strange feeling of being drawn to the ship he saw leaving Mokha just as he was arriving.

If they had actually met, would his friend even recognize him after these ten years? And what would he say to him if he met him? Henry was looking for him, the agent tells him. Perhaps his family had hung their hopes on Henry's trip, and maybe Henry was even more keen than Abdullah was to find him, or at least to uncover some evidence of his friend's whereabouts. Maybe, he thinks, there is no use even pondering all this, for Henry has left without getting the opportunity to meet.

Abdullah feels he has learned enough and, after thanking the agent for the coffee and the travel offer, he takes his leave and returns to the port to prepare for their departure.

Abdullah returns to Mirbat feeling empty, his hopes dashed. But disappointment brings with it a fresh clarity, the kind that, in acceptance of fate, leads a last to a soothing of the soul.

Not his usual self, he is silent for most of the return trip. He avoids spending time with sailors, though his normal bent is to joke and sing with them. Now, he takes a spot near the large mast at the bow of the ship, his mind distracted and always busy. His eyes search the horizon as he mumbles unintelligibly, as if speaking to someone unseen. Yahya approaches him, sensing how Abdullah is feeling. His last-minute visit to the office of the American agent has left him in shock. Something deep inside him has been rudely awakened.

Abdullah reads Yahya's questioning eyes and immediately answers that he has made up his mind to cease even considering to return. Days before, he found himself at a crossroads when the agent offered him an opportunity to return with him. But now, after deep and careful contemplation, he knows where his future lies. It is here in these lands and seas, whose air he has inhaled into his soul. He can no longer imagine another homeland.

Yahya does not speak a word. It is enough for Abdullah to know that someone is listening. Yahya now turns to his friend with compassion and asks him to listen to what he has to say this time.

"Your sense of dashed hopes is an indication of your passion for life and high expectations from the world, but you, only you, can shape your future. If you want to stay here or return there, don't let anyone decide that for you. Just be yourself, Abdullah, not how others want you to be.

"Don't be like the one in the story whose father wanted him to be a great leader, or whose wealthy mother wanted him to be a prominent tradesman, while his cousin wanted him to promise to be a daring warrior like him. The same with his teacher, who saw in him an illustrious thinker. Everyone looked at him as a mirror; they saw only themselves in it. Fed up with all these expectations, the poor young man withdrew from these people and spent his life among a bunch of madmen who were simply being who they were, not what others wished them to be. Some old friends visited him in the asylum and poked fun. He responded, 'You laugh at me because I am different from you, but it is I who should be laughing at you, because you are all alike in my eyes.'" There is nothing left to say after those words.

The *Sharifa* arrives in Mirbat, and Yahya relates the details of the journey to Bin Aqeel, including what happened to Abdullah. At this point, Bin Aqeel is convinced that Abdullah is ready to get married and settle down.

Chapter Eight

Within two months of the return of the *Sharifa* to Mirbat, another ship arrives in Salem on the other side of the world, also returning from Mokha. As the port workers start to unload its cargo, its sailors disembark and head for the families who long to see them after a six- or seven-month absence. One passenger, though, takes a detour, heading west to a modest home atop a small hill, with one last mission to complete before going home.

Henry reaches the home of his friend to find Faith Paul sitting on the porch. As soon as she sees him, the poor woman jumps to her feet to welcome him warmly. In his remorse over what happened to their only son, her husband turned more and more to drink, and now comes home late every night after carousing away his pay, leaving them poorer than ever, and collapses wordlessly into bed. Henry has become her mainstay, cheering her and helping her with her needs when he can.

Henry smiles, knowing he is bearing good news indeed. Until now, his seafaring life has been limited to the Americas; this was his first trip to Yemen and by far the longest voyage. His family had not been happy about him undertaking it, but his desire to somehow ascertain John's situation, awakened every time he saw his friend's mother, made him resolute about accepting a job aboard a ship bound for Mokha.

"Did you see him?" Faith shouts before he reaches her porch, anxious to have her one burning question answered.

"No, I did not see him, but I know that he is alive and living a good life."

She exhales loudly and puts a hand to her chest, closing her eyes against the tears. She is both disappointed and overwhelmingly relieved.

His short answer out of the way, Henry goes on to explain that in Luhayya he chanced upon a young man about the same age as John, named Salim. He had come from the town of Zahraa to sell their farm produce. Salim overheard Henry asking around in the marketplace about an American youth who had been lost in these lands. After verifying the name, age, and description of who he was looking for, Salim told him that he was his friend and knew him well.

"Everyone now calls him Abdullah; it's a common name among the Muslims over there," Henry said, gently, suspecting how this might wound John's mother. He explains that an influential horse trader in Dhofar named Bin Aqeel had taken him in as his son and given him that name. "He lives with him in the region of Mirbat. It's a place famous for exporting frankincense, like the wise men brought to the Christ child in the Bible."

Mirbat, Dhofar, horses, frankincense, Abdullah, Salim, Bin Aqeel—the foreign names and words feel overwhelming to Faith, as Henry tries to built a connection for her between Salem and her son's life in the Arab lands.

As she listens, her heart begins to settle a little as she contemplates her son's new name and life. Henry describes what Salim told him about he'd met John in Luhayya and how they would play together, taking turns leading a camel by a rope while the other rode. A gentle smile creeps onto Faith's face as she hears this. Henry tells her how the two boys would sit in the sand in front of Salim's home on the Red Sea—yes, also as described in the Bible—and about how Salim's family hosted John in their home years later, and about their conversation on what they feared the most.

Suddenly, Henry stops speaking, holding back something he does not want to reveal. But Faith's questioning look gives him no chance to retract the thought. Haltingly, he continues: John's worst fear was that he would forget his mother's face.

At this, her face crumples. "Oh dear Lord, bless my poor boy, shed your mercy upon him, and guide him in Thy ways, that he may love You and come home to his family one day. But Thy will be done," she prays aloud, tears streaming down her face.

Henry bows his head at these words, then looks up at Mrs. Paul and tells her he will come back later, after he has seen his own family.

"Of course," she replies through her tears. "And thank you, dear boy. Your words mean more than you can ever know."

She sits down on the rocking chair on the front porch as Henry departs and speaks again, this time to John himself.

"The wait has been long, my dear boy, but my dream of you will not end. I will wait for you until the day I die. However long you are gone, I shall wait behind the kitchen door, wait for you to come home just as you used to do every evening, to tell you to wash your hands and come down for dinner. When I see the clouds forming and reforming in a sunny sky, I will think of you in my mind's eye, and pray that you are living a full and honorable life. And when the time comes for us to meet, in this life or the next, there will be so much for us to talk about. Someday, we will fill in the blanks of what we left behind."

Henry returns home to greet his anxiously waiting family, while Faith returns to her past sorrows, her heart torn apart by the long vigil. Henry wonders: would she rather have heard that her son had died so the pain would end? Will knowing for certain he is alive and well only lead to a new, everlasting pain? Will she ever find solace? Every other family that lost a loved one on the *Essex* has gone on with their lives, seemingly forgetting that tragedy. But forgetting is not an option for John's mother.

Faith contemplates the picture Henry has given her of her son sitting with his friend, together dipping their feet in the warm Red Sea. She imagines herself sitting with them, dangling her feet in the sea, too, then placing a kiss on her son's head so that he might remember her face forever. Her heart breaks as she recalls her son's worst fear. Her husband's words as her son was preparing for the journey come to her mind. *He will be gone for a moment, then he'll be back.* What is "a moment" can be measured only by the person who is waiting.

Abdullah's marriage contract with Salma is concluded. On the wedding night, his mother Sayyida Khadija dances to the sounds of the *bara'a*. Young men, too, bounce lightly with the steps of the *bara'a*, celebrating Abdullah's happiness. The guests line up to watch the dancers, who pluck their ceremonial daggers from the ground and jump, two at a time, moving in a circle to the harmonious sounds of reed pipes and drums, the polished daggers sparkling as they are waved in the air. The contract is drawn up in the nearby mosque, followed by coffee and sweets for the guests.

Bin Aqeel is the first to congratulate and embrace his son, wishing him great blessings, followed by his uncle Yahya and the rest of the guests, in an atmosphere fragrant with frankincense and myrrh.

At that moment, on the other side of the earth, his mother smiles, comforted as Henry stops by to ask how she is and to assure her again that John is well cared-for by his new family. He suggests, gently, that she might find peace in being glad for him and accepting of where God has placed him.

That evening, the Sayyid prepares a magnificent banquet for the people of Mirbat, who came from all around to congratulate Abdullah and share Bin Aqeel's buffet in front of his home, making sure the poor eat before the rich, the young before the old, and the slave before the freeman, hoping for blessings and heavenly rewards.

Abdullah and Salma are the happiest of newlyweds as they begin life together in their small home adjacent to his father's large house. The couple enjoys the cool fall air in Dhofar, at a magical time when the ground is carpeted in green and Samhan Mountain, hugging the sea coast, is shrouded in fog, adding to its splendor and majesty.

LOST SON OF SALEM: AN AMERICAN BOY'S ODYSSEY IN THE ARAB WORLD

The chilly breeze swirls the fog over Mirbat, causing a refreshing mist to fall on the amorous pair one morning as they walk together. Abdullah ponders Salma's face, her small Belushi nose dampened by the rain, a few drops falling on her lips. He pinches her nose to make sure he is not dreaming. She pushes his hand away from her face and begins to run like a child in the rain, which has now become a downpour. They race together like two canaries just released from a cage, joyfully paired in their love of this place and each other. Nothing can spoil these moments together now but the knowledge that it is just a matter of time before Abdullah takes to the sea again and must be away from his love.

Bin Aqeel continues his strong and sophisticated management of the region of Dhofar. He delegates men to seek the fealty of neighboring tribes, manage their affairs, and care for their livelihood, exploiting any gaps in others' political influence to solidify his position as the head sayyid of Mirbat. With the English having lifted their ban on his movement and nearby forces preoccupied with fighting each other, he has the freedom to handle these affairs as he likes. He doesn't actually establish a state of the sort known in Muscat, Yemen, or Diriyah, but neither does he harbor the kind of political aspirations exhibited by the leaders of those regions. At heart, he is a tradesman, interested in buying and selling and seeking a profit. He funds his rule in Mirbat through his flourishing businesses, with the able assistance of Yahya and Abdullah. The son now loathes being away from Salma for too long and excuses himself from any of his father's maritime journeys to India or the coast of Africa. He refuses to travel any further than Aden or Muscat.

In 1816, he makes a trip to Muscat unlike any other. He has the opportunity to see Rahmah bin Jabir up close—the man infamous for his aggression and tyranny against his adversaries, especially his cousins of the Khalifah clan. He is shifting his loyalty now, and has come to Muscat to explore the possibility of an amicable relationship with

Al-Sultan Saeed, a potential ally against the Qasimis and Ibn Saud, with whom he had aligned himself not long ago.

In Dhofar, Bin Aqeel remains on the sidelines of events farther abroad. He continues to deal with the British with extreme caution. The French presence having dwindled, the British are extending their influence and surveying all the ports in the region. It's only a matter of time before they collide with the Qasimis, Ibn Saud's allies, who have never let up on raiding Indian trade ships and combatting the British Navy in a region extending from the Persian Gulf to Mokha in the Red Sea. Their ships, faster and lighter than the Europeans', sometimes take them almost as far as Bombay. The Qasimis had been a force to be reckoned with in years past, with a naval fleet that exceeded sixty large ships and numerous smaller ones, sufficient to carry more than twenty thousand men.

In 1817, Bin Aqeel receives a letter from Abdulrahman informing him that Al-Sharif Hamoud, the ruler of Abu Arish, has been killed in battle after forming a temporary alliance with his adversaries, the rulers of Asir, against their new shared enemy, the Turks. Bin Aqeel reminisces over his old ally and prays for God's mercy on him. He will never forget their sometimes fraught years of cooperation, from the doomed sale of the island of Kamaran to participating in Al-Sharif's military campaign against his enemies.

But, he wonders, what are the Turks doing in the southern regions, after leaving the area decades before? The Turks are expanding into the land of Hijaz, reaching south into Asir, paving a way to power in the heart of the Arabian Peninsula and arriving at Ibn Saud's home in Diriyah, in the center of Najd. The Turks are sure to protect their backs against any reinforcements coming from his followers there.

The new Ottoman leader in Cairo, Muhammad Ali Pasha, has been tightening his grip on Egypt ever since removing the Mamelukes from power, in the citadel massacre that killed a thousand of them. He is now supervising these campaigns, waging a proxy war on behalf of Topkapi

Palace to combat Ibn Saud and his Wahhabist movement, which has spread to the Hijaz, Yemen, Asir, and the frontiers of Iraq and the Levant. Ibn Saud's control of Hijaz has threatened the Ottoman Empire's religious leadership.

Within a year after Al-Sharif Hamoud's death, Bin Aqeel receives the news of the fall of Diriyah, which has been demolished by Ibrahim Pasha's forces. This marks the end of Ibn Saud's reign and leaves the region vulnerable to tribal conflicts.

Bin Aqeel's expanding commercial activities include a trade in horses that he has delegated to Abdullah. He hesitated about this, knowing Abdullah's intense passion for horses, for he usually makes it a practice not to delegate a matter to someone who might be swayed in his judgment of sales offers.

The horse trade flourished in Mirbat's ancient market two centuries ago, before the Portuguese tried to sabotage it to weaken the Arab kingdoms in the Persian Gulf. It is said the name Mirbat comes from "marbat," a horse rein, since so many purebred Arabian horses came from there. Buyers would come to Mirbat from all across the peninsula, then re-sell the horses in India and China.

The autumn weather in Dhofar ensured ample feed for horses, whether they are bred for riding and transport or for warfare. Abdullah has a passion for chasing the wind on the backs of the most spirited steeds. He suggests to his father that he travel to Ras Al-Khaimah to meet Shaykh Sultan Bin Saqr, to ask for the two elite horses he had promised to give him in return for his passage on the ship from Mokha. These horses, he argues, would be a valuable addition to his stable, and who knows what benefit could come from them?

Bin Aqeel does not appear enthusiastic about Abdullah's request; the horse trade is a trifling fraction of his business, but with Abdullah's persistence, he grudgingly agrees.

Abdullah departs on a small *sunbooq* owned by his father and heads for Ras al-Khaimah, this time unconcerned with what fate may have in store for him. He bids farewell to his father, then to his wife, as is his habit. He is surprised by Salma's tight grip on his hands. She doesn't want him to go. She is not convinced of this mission; her heart tells her that something bad may happen to her husband. She has been noticing the signs of pregnancy, but has not yet told him.

It is the fall of 1819 when Abdullah arrives in Muscat and notices there a heavy presence of the British navy, the likes of which he has not seen before. The ships seem to be preparing for something. He stays for a week in Muscat, but is unable to sail farther. The British are now blocking passage through the Strait of Hormuz of any ships that do not raise the British flag. News travels among the sailors in the port that the British are preparing to wage a major war on Ras al-Khaimah, taking advantage of the enmity between the Qasimis and Al-Sultan Saeed, following the Turks' victory over Ibn Saud, the Qasimis' ally. They aim to entrench their hegemony in the region and bring the Persian Gulf under British rule. The British had hoped for the support of the Turkish forces in Egypt, but a delegate sent to meet with Ibrahim Pasha on his way home found he was not interested in aiding the British in this endeavor. The only one left to exploit for their own interests is the Sultan of Oman, thanks to his hostility to the Qasimis. '

Given the situation, Abdullah's mission now appears next to impossible, but he does not want to return empty-handed. Driven by youthful enthusiasm and his obsession to obtain those horses, he decides to find a guide willing to take him by land to reach his goal. He knows how dangerous it is to travel by land in a region rife with conflict, with the war drums already beating near the coast, but the excitement of this plan makes him dismiss the risks. It will just be a few days, he thinks, before he reaches Sharjah or Ras al-Khaimah, gets what he wants from the shaykh, and returns.

Abdullah hires an Omani guide and departs with him on camelback to Ras al-Khaimah by way of Al-Batinah. The caravan passes through Shinas, at the northernmost end of the coastal plains, where he sees mangroves lining the city's delta, reminding him of Luhayya. He thinks of his friend Salim, and how long it has been since he saw him and mother and brothers last—already seven years since he left them planning their move to Al-Zahraa. He wonders how they are now, since Al-Sharif, who planted the town, was killed. He vows to pay him a visit next time he goes there.

The guide senses someone is following them. He was reluctant to come to this area, because Shinas has been the site of recent battles between Ibn Saud's forces on one side and the Omanis and British on the other. The camel riders have barely passed Shinas when a small armed troop from Ibn Saud's guards block their path and arrest them, accusing Abdullah of being a British spy, which his blue eyes and golden hair clearly suggest. His deep tan from the Arabian sun and fluent Arabic dialect from Dhofar fail to dissuade them from this assertion, and making things worse is that his guide is a subject of the Sultan, who harbors hostility towards their shaykhs. They are given no opportunity to explain or persuade the soldiers to believe them.

The troop pushes them north and throws them in jail. Abdullah, bound and shackled, finds himself in an unknown village, which he sees briefly after his guard removes the blindfold over his eyes. There are beautiful houses nestled among groves of palm, lemon, and fig trees, overshadowed by towering mountains. To the east lies a port in a harbor bordered on each side by a rocky point projecting into the water, like bared teeth.

The sound of sailors chanting reaches his ears. They are unloading a ship that has stopped to take on fresh water. "You came from Mukalla and docked at Khor Fakkan," they sing, and Abdullah realizes that he is in Khor Fakkan.

The jail guards call him *Nasrani*, the Christian, in spite of having seen him pray like them, facing their same prayer direction and reciting verses of the Qur'an. These men are more rigid in their beliefs than people he has met in Yemen or in Muscat or Basrah, or any other region. He notices the guards speaking a dialect new to him. He learns later, when listening to them talk among themselves, that they are from central Najd, and that they are what remains of an old garrison that Ibn Saud's army left behind when they invaded Shinas, south of this jail. Being so far from their homeland, they refuse to believe Abdullah when he tells them of Ibn Saud's fate and what happened to Diriyah a few months earlier, at the hands of the Egyptians. Perhaps they simply do not want to believe it. In their eyes, he is just a Christian, a British spy, not worthy of being believed.

Abdullah is held for what he estimates is six months or so, although his guide was let go after a month. He does not see sunlight, save through a small crack at the top of his jail cell. During the night, the only thing that relieves his solitude is the voice of one of the guards reciting the Qur'an in a dewy voice that wafts on the fresh breeze sifting through that one crack. On nights when the moon is visible, he contemplates the full moon in the sky, counting its arrival six times. It shines through the hole in the midnight darkness, revealing the face of his mother in Salem on the moon's surface. Clouds drift across the sky, blocking his view of the moon. He quickly waves his hand as if trying to move the clouds to prevent them from stealing away his mother's image, a picture he has just barely been able to recollect after losing it for many months. He strains his mind to keep her in view and wishes that he had a pen and paper to draw what has settled in his memory of her face, to keep it from disappearing. He is still terrified that his worst fear will come to pass and he will forever lose any semblance of her features in his mind's eye.

One month has passed since Abdullah left. Salma's worries swell, in spite of Bin Aqeel's reassurance that he is not yet due to return. But fate holds something else in store for Salma as she waits. A ship arrives in Mirbat bearing six families coming from the coast of Makran to settle and work in Dhofar. Salma meets a woman who used to work with her mother. The woman tells her about her family, the people from whom she had been kidnapped as a girl. She was a little older at that time than Abdullah was when he left Salem, so she remembers them well, and the Belushi woman had no trouble identifying her. Sayyida Khadija encourages her to send a message to her family on the ship returning to Makran, to assure them of her well-being and invite them to come visit her as soon as possible. Sayyida Khadija instills her with renewed hope that she will see her husband and her family together. Salma says a heartfelt prayer that God will reunite them after this prolonged separation.

But more than seven months pass, far too long for a journey that was supposed to take no more than two or three. Abdullah's family is in turmoil. His father cannot stop thinking about him, and Salma is soon to give birth to her firstborn. Bin Aqeel dreads to think what might have happened to his son. Upon the insistence of his wife and Salma, he sends one of his men to Muscat to investigate, and in due course the man returns to tell them that he has learned Abdullah left with a guide to go overland to Ras al-Khaimah and that no one in Muscat had seen him since.

Abdullah is moved to another jail when the garrison is dismantled and the troops are transferred to Dibba, several miles north of Khor Fakkan, but now the jail is under the Qasimis' administration. The head officer refuses to believe his story that Bin Aqeel is his father and that Abdullah is merely seeking to meet Shaykh Sultan Bin Saqr to collect the horses he was promised. The color of his eyes and golden hair, as well as the narrative told by the guards who brought him that he was a British spy lying in wait for them, make the truth of his story questionable. The guards warn the head officer not to be fooled by his genuine-sounding accent, nor his faithful bowing and prostrating in prayer.

Abdullah languishes in this jail for another two months, closing in on the autumn of 1819. The pain in his thigh from his wound during Al-Sharif's battle returns to him. But lying in the prison in Dibba is not nearly as exhausting as the prison of his memories of Salem. The imprisonment of his body can't compare to the imprisonment of his soul.

How many are imprisoned within four walls, yet their spirits roam free, and how many are free to roam the earth, yet their souls are imprisoned?

One day, news spreads among the guards that the British fleet is preparing to attack the Qasimis, and this soon becomes an overwhelming preoccupation. With the arrival of December's forty-day chill in 1819, three British naval ships arrive at Ras al-Khaimah carrying troops led by Major-General William Keir. Two more ships belonging to Al-Sultan Saeed and ground forces of three thousand strong join the British to attack the Qasimis' center and put a limit on their power.

The shaykhs consult one another about what to do. One officer suggests they use their English captive as a bargaining chip for negotiations. Abdullah's existence comes as a surprise to many: an English prisoner right there in Dibba? Especially since the British have never presented a demand to have him released. They begin asking questions about this prisoner, and the officer explains that the man is always repeating the name of Shaykh Sultan Bin Saqr, claiming he owes him something, and that he is the son of the Sayyid of Dhofar, Muhammad Bin Aqeel. But these tricks and deceptions have never fooled him, the officer proclaims smugly.

Shaykh Sultan's curiosity is piqued, and he leaves quickly for Dibba, where he discovers that the captive is none other than the young man who had long ago helped him travel from Mokha to Muscat. So the story is true! He has Abdullah released immediately and honors him with great hospitality, to the amazement of his jailers. Instead of the two horses he had promised long ago, he gives him twenty of the finest he owns, hoping to compensate him for his long misery and show his gratitude for what Abdullah and his father had done in taking him in good faith on their ship.

Abdullah requests that he be allowed to return with him to Ras al-Khaimah to help defend it from the British fleet, but the shaykh refuses and asks him to leave. He knows the relationship Bin Aqeel has with the Sultan of Oman, and he does not want that to deteriorate even more with his son's involvement in fighting his ships.

So Abdullah returns to Khor Fakkan, accompanied by some of the shaykh's men to ensure his safety, then boards a *sunbooq* the shaykh has ordered to transport him and the horses to Mirbat.

In Ras al-Khaimah, the military operation ends with the Qasimis' defeat. The shaykhs surrender and decide, after seeing the heavy losses their army has suffered, to sign a general peace treaty. In the end, the Aal Khalifa clan of Bahrain also signs on, although Rahmah bin Jabir abstains from being a party to it. The signers, led by Shaykh Sultan bin Saqr, agree to surrender all fortifications, ships, and cannons to General Keir, on condition that his troops cease entering cities to destroy them.

Abdullah arrives in Mirbat after an absence of nearly a year, to find his wife waiting for him with twin baby boys. The months have taken their toll on her, with the fear he might never return to see Sayyida Khadija playing with his sons, about whom it is joked that one is Belushi and the other American. Bin Aqeel holds a magnificent banquet, inviting all of Mirbat, to celebrate his son's safe return, and Sayyida Khadija does her best to make him swear to never travel alone again, or at least to take one of his father's men with him always so someone knows where he is.

That night, the old dream of his mother returns to him. He sees her rising up out of their house's chimney into the sky and disappearing beyond the clouds over the Atlantic, but this time she calls out to him, "So many travelers search the world for something they think they need, but when they return home, they find that what they need has been there all along."

"I promise I will return to you," Abdullah replies. "I will return, if it's the last thing I do in my mortal life."

Chapter Nine

A few months after Abdullah's return to Mirbat, news spread through the town of a boat that has been grounded a little west of Taqah. Bin Aqeel sends one of his men to investigate and discovers that an English ship, *Swallow*, was wrecked near the coast of Dhofar and landed at the nearest beach, which happened to be Taqah. The locals there have jumped at the opportunity the Christians' stranded ship offered and looted it. The ship's captain tried to scare them off with gunshots, but that was not enough, and his sailors weren't up to fighting after having been too long at sea with no food or water.

The locals, angry at being shot at, proceeded to capture all the sailors and steal the contents of the ship, which had been passing from Madras on its way to Aden. On hearing of this incident, Bin Aqeel directs a group of his guards, headed by Abdullah, to rescue the ship's passengers from the locals and return what they looted. He also sends his shipbuilders, *qallafs*, who work on his ships in Mirbat, with stern orders to repair the *Swallow*, whatever the cost, and restore it to working condition.

The released Englishmen spend a few days as guests of Bin Aqeel, who showers them with his generosity while they wait for their ship to be repaired. They then continue on safely to their destination.

The *Swallow's* benevolent rescue does not go unnoticed. When the news of Bin Aqeel's actions reach the government in Bombay, it responds in a way he never expected. Months later, an English military ship arrives in Mirbat, reminding the local folk uneasily of the last time a military ship flying the British flag anchored in their harbor. The ship's captain brings an official letter from the government in Bombay, thanking him for his swift intervention to save the English ship and protect its sailors and return what was stolen, as well as repairing the damage to the ship. The captain also comes bearing gifts, including crates of firearms, to express the government's appreciation and gratitude.

Bin Aqeel knows the English had long ago stopped pursuing his arrest, but rewarding him with gifts and arms was a reversal of interests that had never occurred to him possible. Not everyone in Bombay had agreed with so rewarding Bin Aqeel; some still insisted that he was a fugitive from justice and should be tried for what he did to the *Essex* and the death of Captain Carter, but those voices were unable to stand up to the stronger camp led by his former ally, Mr. Duncan. This group knows that by giving arms to Bin Aqeel, an ally of the Sultan of Oman, they are paving the way to cementing their power in the Arabian Sea after the treaty with the Qasamis effectively subdued the Gulf ports.

As for the Arabian Peninsula, its borders have been conquered by the Ottomans, thanks to their governor in Egypt. But the heart of the Peninsula remains rife with conflicts since Ibrahim Pasha's destruction of Diriyah and imprisonment of its ruler left a political void.

Bin Aqeel takes advantage of the Bombay government's offers by diverting a portion of his trade to India, in return for customs discounts on his merchandise. His business with coastal cities in India begins to thrive, especially around Cochin and Madras.

Bin Aqeel has no shortage of new markets and new and bigger ships, but his interests gradually move from his expert trading and market success to political aspirations. After years of buying and selling, he seeks an office befitting of his stature. He turns his sights towards Egypt, whose influence has infiltrated deep within the Peninsula. Sayyida Khadija does not like these aims. She knows well the problems they face every time her husband enters into political matters. The best times she has shared with her husband were when he was a trader—and only a trader.

Bin Aqeel and Abdullah depart on one of his ships headed for Jiddah, carrying with it the finest gifts he had brought from Bombay, Zanzibar, and Muscat, to give to the Egyptian governor. Another ship accompanies this voyage to provide support and protection. Yahya, his wife's uncle, has stayed behind to care for his family. Abdullah had hoped to stop in Luhayya to look for Salim, but his father's orders are to stop only in Aden, to restock supplies.

The vessel arrives in Jiddah at the beginning of the month of Ramadan in 1823. The ship stays only a short time, but it is enough for Abdullah to admire its many-storied houses with protruding window frames covered in intricately carved wooden latticework, something new to his eyes. Bin Aqeel and his small caravan, comprising his son and some of his men and slaves, head for Makkah to perform the *umrah*. The weather is rather hot in early summer, but the evening's refreshing breezes cool their bodies as they walk together, wrapped in the simple white sheets of the *ihram*, helping the travelers step up the pace as they arrive at the holy house of God. At the Grand Mosque, where the Kaaba is situated, they perform the *umrah*, the seven circuits around the Kaaba, then split up to find places to rest.

Abdullah sits down against one of the mosque's pillars to recite some verses of the Qur'an from the volume his wife had presented him as a gift, which he has carried with him ever since he returned from Ras al-Khaimah. He ponders the people who have come from all corners of the earth to circumambulate the ancient house and cling to the door of the Kaaba, beseeching the Lord of the House. As soon as the prescribed prayer is completed, the worshippers throng the area around the cubic structure, reaching for its drapes, lilting and swaying like boats surrounding an island and looking to anchor.

The holy sites are now under the control of the Topkapi Palace government after the fall of Ibn Saud. Both sides of the conflict are

Muslims praying towards one qibla, one direction of prayer, but the Arab personality in central Najd is not like that of Istanbul, just as the dwellers of Mikhlaf differ from the residents of Basrah. The religion he learned in his parents' home in Mirbat, where a tomb enshrines its founder, is closer to Sufism and the holiness the pilgrim feels here in Makkah, and far removed from the severity he saw among his jail guards in Khor Fakkan, who refused to even return his greeting of peace, arguing that he was a Christian even though he prayed just as they did.

Religion for most people, he surmises, is determined by their place of birth and childhood years, then reshaped by the conditions of their current location. He was certainly proof of that. He was born into a Protestant Christian home in his birthplace in Massachusetts, but he grew up to be a Muslim when he moved at a young age into an Arab Muslim home. His short life has taught him to trust those who seek the truth and doubt those who claim to have found it.

One of his father's slaves tells him he is to come immediately. His father is preparing to travel to Taif to meet the Pasha of Makkah there, leaving after they have their pre-dawn meal.

In Taif, Bin Aqeel meets with Ahmad Pasha, the ruler of Hijaz. They share the iftar, the sunset meal to break the fast, in the man's home that same day. Ahmad Pasha is the nephew of Muhammad Ali Pasha, who appointed him as his deputy after his son, Ibrahim, withdrew from the Arabian Peninsula, and delegated him to watch over his forces in Asir. The Pasha shows Bin Aqeel a letter from his uncle, confirming his desire for the Hijaz region to secede and be ruled independently from the Ottoman government based at Topkapi Palace, particularly after his success in the central Peninsula.

The Pasha's words embolden Bin Aqeel in his hopes of securing a government position from the governor in Egypt. Ahmad Pasha, aware of Bin Aqeel's past relationship with Al-Sharif Hamoud and participation in his military campaigns in Mikhlaf, as well as his

familiarity with tribal leaders, consults him on his campaign against
Asir. Bin Aqeel isn't particularly interested in giving advice and focuses
on the purpose of his trip to Egypt, namely to meet the governor and
present him some gifts.

After their one night in Taif, Bin Aqeel heads back to Makkah
to meet with some influential locals who have expressed grievances
against the pasha. He asks them to put their complaints into writing
to take with him to Egypt and be presented to Muhammad Ali for his
deliberation.

The ship sets sail once again from Jiddah, traveling north past
Yanbu, the port where visitors to Madinah, the City of the Prophet,
alight before making the five-day trek to the city east of the port. Most
ships travelling between Suez and Jiddah anchor here, but theirs does
not stop; it continues on past Al-Wajh and nears Al-Nouman Island
in the northern Red Sea before turning left toward the Gulf of Suez,
eventually reaching the port of Suez. This is the most northern point in
the Red Sea to which Abdullah has ever sailed.

An escort sent by the pasha has been waiting for them in Suez to
facilitate their land journey across Egypt to Cairo. The slaves unload
the ship's cargo of gifts and reload them onto camels, which will also
bear Bin Aqeel, Abdullah, and some assistants onward. Some guards
remain to protect the ship until their return.

The caravan arrives at night and heads for the lodging prepared
for the pasha's guests in Al-Azbakeyah, at the heart of the capital and
center of the ruling class. Here, in its square, Muhammad Ali Pasha was
sworn in as governor of Egypt in 1805, the same year that Abdullah
left his family in Salem on the *Essex* heading for Yemen. The travelers
wearily fall asleep in bedchambers carefully prepared to receive them at
the end of a long day of travel.

Abdullah awakens to the sound of the *azan*, the call to prayer,
reverberating within the walls of the ancient city. Dozens of voices mix
in a melodic cacophony resounding from minarets scattered around

them in every direction, echoing across Cairo's glorious skies. The feeling he had the first time he heard the *azan* with Captain Joseph Orne in Luhayya comes over him in a wave, and he has a sensation of grasping the long chain of memories stretching behind him all the way to Salem. He sees the faces of the *Essex's* crew and remembers its captain and sailors. Leon, the ship's cook, comes to his mind, the man who had lived alone and died alone in a strange land.

His reverie is broken as his father wakes the others for prayer. By the time the sun is rising above the horizon, Bin Aqeel is preparing for his meeting with the pasha in his palace in the Cairo Citadel.

Abdullah seizes this opportunity to explore the city streets and quarters. Cairo feels like another world. He has visited Yemen and lived in Dhofar, stayed in Muscat, stopped in Jiddah, and traded in Basrah, but he has never seen an Arab city quite like Cairo, or the magnificent Nile upon which it is set. He is impressed by the long, wide streets and spotless roads, the grand architecture, and the multitude of mosques. He walks along the road built by the French from Al-Azbakeyah to Boulaq, after passing over the Maghribi bridge. He hires a guide, along with some of his father's men, to go west to see the three Giza pyramids and the massive form of the Great Sphinx, its chest recently cleared of the statue's accumulation of sand. On their way back, they pass by a printing house and ironwork and carpentry workshops that supply parts to manufacture weapons and battle tools; textile factories and weavers of silk, rugs, and tents; and manufacturers of saddles, copper pots, paper, and wooden ornaments.

Abdullah returns to the guest house that day feeling as if he has lived through a dream, wandering through a mythical city, the kind his mother used to tell him bedtime stories about.

Bin Aqeel has met with the governor at the citadel at Mokattam and presented his gifts, which the latter gratefully accepted and reciprocated with gifts for the visitor. Bin Aqeel also delivers the letters from the Makkah leaders, expressing their grievances with the Pasha of Makkah.

But Bin Aqeel has not succeeded in getting a promise of a political post in the regions under the pasha's power in the Arabian Peninsula. The pasha, at the moment, is preoccupied with responding to a request from the caliph Mahmud II for help in quelling the revolutionaries in the Greek region of Morea.

The conversation and relationship with the Ottoman caliphate, he tells Abdullah, remind him of his old friend, Al-Sharif Hamoud, and his relationship with Ibn Saud. Both enjoyed their share of sophistication and cunning in handling their adversaries and allies. The pasha is waging wars on behalf of Topkapi Palace but at the same time building a modern state, working to separate Egyptian politics from Ottoman politics, even if that leads to a war with the sovereign government itself.

The governor's representative takes Bin Aqeel on a tour of the new city the pasha has founded. His focus is on education, so he has opened many schools and colleges and even sent students to Europe. He has also established military institutes, such as the cavalry and artillery school, and built hospitals and corresponding medical institutes such as Al-Qasr Al-Ayni and a childbirth school for midwives. He has prioritized manufacturing and built factories for textiles, cotton ginning, and oil extraction, often replacing outdated methods with new steam-powered mechanical tools.

The deputy takes him by the ship-building basin that the pasha ordered built after commencing his campaign in Najd, intending it to become Egypt's core naval fleet building site. The governor's deputy advisor recognizes the awe in Bin Aqeel's eyes and says, "Not many people see things as they are and ponder why they are so; even fewer dream of things that have not come into existence and ask why not. The rest have no thoughts, either way. ... Under the tutelage of our leader, the pasha, we nurture those who dream and teach those who ask, and we kindle the flame of inquisitiveness in the rest."

After Bin Aqeel's return from Egypt, he waits in vain for an answer from the governor to his request. Finally, he is convinced that his political ambitions will not play out by way of Egypt. He returns his attention to growing his business and governing Dhofar, with its coasts and mountains, trying to create some degree of the urbanization he witnessed in Egypt. He establishes Salalah, not far from Mirbat, as the capital for his area of influence and builds a residence and administrative buildings there on the Cairo model.

Abdullah admires his father's ability to deftly switch between the roles of politician and businessman, though it's one of the things he can't quite understand about Bin Aqeel's personality. He has absorbed his father's passion for discovery, travel and adventure, but he has no inclination toward governance and politics. His first love is his little family and the horses he has taught his children to ride and care for.

One spring evening in 1829, five years after their return from Egypt, Bin Aqeel is returning along a tranquil beach to Salalah from a visit in Mirbat, accompanied by a small group of his slaves, when a shot rings out. It flies from the direction of a nearby mountain to land squarely in Bin Aqeel's chest, puncturing the *qamees* his wife had given him just days before his trip. The slaves hardly have a chance to realize what happened to their master before they are ambushed from behind. A fight breaks out, resulting in the death of some of the slaves and the escape of others.

Bin Aqeel's soul returns to his Creator on the land he loved, his blood pouring out on the beach and mixing with the sea water on which he loved to travel.

The news of Bin Aqeel's murder reaches his wife, Sayyida Khadija, in Mirbat. Those first days of disbelief and grief would have been agony if not for her strong faith in her Lord, and having Salma by her side, along with her uncle Yahya, who rushed back to Mirbat to console the

Sayyid's family. The Sayyida knew better than anyone else the dangers that awaited her husband every time he embarked on a sea voyage or rushed to mount a horse. *Sometimes death is not the worst calamity; rather, living in wait of it is.*

As news of Bin Aqeel's death reaches Muscat, Al-Sultan Saeed sends a battalion to ensure the security of Dhofar and prevent any disturbances that could arise out of the political vacuum left by his demise. He also sends a message to Bin Aqeel's brother, Abdulrahman, in Bombay at the time, to ask whether he might be interested in assuming his brother's post. But Abdulrahman declines the sultan's proposal, saying he had no political aspirations. He has learned enough from his brother's experience what politics can bring upon a person.

Just one person has not yet received the news: Abdullah. He has been in Cochin, India, purchasing spices. The moment his ship arrives in Muscat to unload its cargo, the sultan sends his delegate to inform him of the sad news and invite him to meet the sultan, who wishes to offer his condolences in person. Although not deeply bonded with Bin Aqeel, the sad news still stings Abdullah, stirring a mix of unexpected emotions and a subtle ache for the lost chance to deepen their relationship.

Al-Sultan Saeed meets Abdullah in the same office where he had met his father twenty-three years before. The sultan is not much older than Abdullah, maybe five or six years. Meeting him personally for the first time, Abdullah recalls how his father used to admire the youthful sultan's personality, back when he first took over the reins of the government in Muscat. Much has changed since then. The Sultan of Oman's influence has spread, as Bin Aqeel had predicted when he first met him; the Omani empire now reaches from Bandar Abbas, Bandar Lengeh, Qeshm, and Hormuz on the banks of the Persian Gulf, to Zanzibar, Mombasa, and Mogadishu on the eastern coast of Africa, which he rules with a firm grip. The sultan has worked to develop free trade with various countries and built massive trade fleets supported by a sophisticated naval force, unmatched in strength except for the British navy, to protect travel between the two parts of his reign in Oman and the African coast.

After offering his condolences and mentioning Bin Aqeel's skillful management of Dhofar, the sultan surprises Abdullah by asking him to work on his sea fleet, to command one of the sultan's ships headed for Mombasa and participate in quelling an uprising there against the Omanis.

The sultan is aware of Abdullah's navigation skills; that he accompanied his deceased father many times and gained experience on the high seas and on the battlefield. This seems a good opportunity to consolidate his allies' loyalty. Abdullah accepts without hesitation. After all, he is a subject of the sultan, raised in the land of Dhofar, and cannot refuse. But first he asks permission to visit his family in Mirbat and console Sayyida Khadija.

Abdullah departs on the *Liverpool,* which bears sixty-four cannons, with one hundred and fifty sailors under his command and several Omani naval officers. This is the first time he has embarked on a ship with such destructive capacity. He stands at the bow of the ship as it sails out flanked by two frigates, with two smaller military ships not far away, followed by small supply boats. His golden locks flutter over his shoulders as his blue eyes glint with the setting sun. If not for the Omani turban wrapping his head and the *janbiyyah* dagger fastened on the belt around his waist, one might think he was a Viking ruler sallying forth to expand his kingdom. His spirits fly high as he sees all this firepower moving at maximum speed, all subject to his guidance.

That exuberance fades quickly when he recalls the little wooden boat he used to play with on Derby Wharf in Salem with his friend Henry, and how he used his shirt to make a sail that would propel the little boat under vendors' carts. He remembers his mother's bedtime stories about great conquerors. How he wishes she could see him now, with this whole fleet under his direction! He imagines standing near her on the *Liverpool*. He sees her and she sees him, he hears her and she hears him, he comes closer and smells that familiar scent. He tries to conjure up her image as it was implanted in his memory as a child, but the passage of days and years has blurred that image. He strives with all his might to retain what is left of her in his mind.

Abdullah arrives in Mirbat overwhelmed by his memories of Bin Aqeel. He lowers a small boat from the *Liverpool* and heads for the shore with a few soldiers. *The town hasn't changed at all*, he muses as he approaches his home. *We are the ones that have changed. We have gotten older and the place has stayed the same.*

Countless people have come and gone from this place. Abdullah himself is now in his thirties. His hair has grown long, his weight has increased, and his appearance has changed. He can easily list all the things that have changed within him, but he presumes there must be something that has not, that will always remain at the core of his being. But what would that be?

He recalls a story he read in Bin Aqeel's library about an old ship anchored at a port waiting for repairs. The workers remove some old parts and replace them with new ones, but the process drags on and, in the end, all parts of the ship are replaced with new ones. While working, the repairmen pile up the old parts in an empty plot of land, where another group of workers takes these leftover old parts and use them to build another ship. Once the repairs are completed, there are two ships. When the ship owner comes, he asks which ship is his: the ship whose parts were all replaced with new parts, or the ship made up of the old parts?

Abdullah is at a crossroads in his life. He asks himself the same question: Who am I? He had thought this question resolved long ago, but the death of Bin Aqeel has stirred up conflicting feelings, awakened a dormant yearning. Is he John Herman Paul from Massachusetts, or is he Abdullah bin Muhammad Bin Aqeel from Dhofar? As the small boat approaches the shore, he stops thinking about this and turns his thoughts to Sayyida Khadija.

Upon reaching the house, he seizes her hands and kisses them as her tears flow. She is surprised and gladdened by his unexpected return. Seeing him now takes her back in time, to the terrified moment in Kamaran when she had spared the little boy from the hands of Bin Aqeel's men as they were about to kill him. He is the son she did not give birth to, and he is now the only one remaining for her in this world, her solace and consolation.

As soon as she loosens her grip on him, he heads for Salma, kissing the nose he had always pinched when teasing her, then rushes to greet his sons, who are now about the age he was when he first came to Yemen on the *Essex*. Seeing them now, he remembers that arrival. Could it really be a quarter of century?

Returning to his family home, he feels like a branch taken from a tree that has returned to its roots. It is said that a stick cut from a tree in a forest to be made into a flute feels the pain of separation and begins to wail, so the person who cut it feels pity for it and opens some holes in it to let it vent its sadness. And from then on, the stick never stops its sighing.

Abdullah stays for two days and one night. He meets Salma's mother and brothers, who have come from the coast of Makran to be reunited with their daughter after their long separation. He sees in his wife's eyes her joy at watching her mother play with her grandchildren. He wonders if fate will ever grant him the same joy. He visits his father's grave and prays for mercy on his soul. *The deceased are kept alive in the memories of the living. When a relative or friend or lover dies, a part of us dies with as well, but our departed ones are not really dead until we forget them.*

Then, reluctantly, Abdullah boards a boat to rejoin the fleet anchored near Mirbat, to complete the mission the sultan commissioned him to do. He gazes toward the town until it fades from view, remembering his voyages with his father. His mind whirls with questions about those he has bid farewell to, and those that bade farewell to him. Did he leave them behind, or have they left him behind? Where is his homeland: the one he left, or the one he arrived at?

He senses memory itself slipping away from him. He struggles to remember people and events and times. In this, his one comfort, ironic as it might be, is that when memory fades, it's possible to enjoy the same beautiful thing repeatedly, as if it was occurring for the first time.

The sultan's forces reach Mombasa and battle with the rebels in a short and swift war, succeeding in clearing the city and restoring the African portion of the sultanate. They then move south to Zanzibar, to tighten its power there. During that campaign, Abdullah sustains a minor injury that he recovers quickly from, but the pain from his old wound from Al-Sharif Hamoud's war returns with a vengeance. He finds himself bedridden, with no strength to move.

Some of the Omani fleet's vessels remain anchored in Zanzibar after things have settled down in the sultanate's favor, but the *Liverpool* returns to Muscat without its commander. While waiting for the pain to subside, Abdullah takes up residence in the ancient Castle of the Arabs, built by the Omanis for its proximity to the sultan's palace. On the days he feels better, his assistant helps prop him up against the castle's western wall, where he can watch the ships as they come and go in the nearby port.

Coconut palm fields proliferate on Zanzibar island, known for its temperate climate and fertile soil, but what most sets this place apart, along with Pemba island, which neighbors it off the coast of Africa, is its clove plantations. Sultan Saeed brought seedlings for this Southeast Asian tree to Zanzibar, which consequently became an important resource for the island's economy. Ships come to its famous port from all over the world seeking out this precious spice.

Sitting against the castle's wall, Abdullah sips his morning coffee, enhanced with the delicious scent of cloves. His assistant prepares the cup with a fresh grinding of clove buds harvested earlier in the year near his residence.

Abdullah's assistant welcomes the signs that his leader's health is improving, hoping that their return to Oman and his return to his family in Sohar is imminent. Abdullah asks his companion to remind him of the reason they came here, to which he answers, bewildered, "Was it not to quell the rebels who tried to seize power?" Abdullah looks into his coffee cup, mumbling something his companion cannot understand. "But I am here due to this plant and its strong aroma. This is what brought me here from Salem."

About two months after Abdullah's arrival in Zanzibar, a messenger from the office of the American Agency comes to inform him that the captain of an American ship wishes to meet him before it returns to the United States. Abdullah agrees to meet the captain and invites him to come the next day. He spends the night thinking of all the times in the past he has been on the verge of meeting someone from the American continent.

The first came twenty years before, when Captain Nicola offered to smuggle him away, still a fearful youth on the ship called the *Falak*, but then Bin Aqeel's sudden decision to embark early foiled his plans. The second was fifteen years ago, when his arrival in Mokha coincided with the departure of an American ship. Even then, he was still young, lost and hesitant, and could not make all of his own decisions. By then he knew no other family or homeland than the house of Bin Aqeel, which had embraced and nurtured him.

But now he is his own master. Lying alone on a pallet in the open air in the center of the castle, he wonders what tomorrow has in store. He gazes at the stars in the clear sky, with nothing to disturb the peace other than the misgivings weighing heavily on his thoughts. Falling into a fitful sleep, he is visited by the specter of his mother again, but with a new scenario. This time, his mother appears to be giving birth to him anew. Wrapping him in a white cloth, she takes him in her arms to suckle him.

This vision stays with him as he wakes before the sun rises. He washes up to pray the dawn prayer on his cushion. The sound of the imam's recitation breaks through the darkness: "*And the heart of the mother of Moses became void, and she would have betrayed him if We had not fortified her heart, that she might be of the believers.*"

In the early morning, three men come to visit, one of whom he judges by his clothing to be the captain. With him is an older man who looks intently at Abdullah, as if inspecting him. The third man introduces himself as the officer in charge of the American Agency in Zanzibar, which his government has negotiated with the sultan to become a permanent consulate. Abdullah remains stretched out on his pallet, his bad leg preventing him from standing to welcome his guests. His assistant has arranged some wooden chairs around him and goes to fetch coffee, while Abdullah invites them to be seated.

The captain begins by asking questions to confirm Abdullah's identity, but his poorly remembered English makes it difficult to communicate. He tries answering in Arabic, which none of the visitors understand. Then he tries Swahili, which so happens to be well understood by the agency officer. He confirms it to the others: he is indeed Abdullah bin Muhammad Bin Aqeel from Mirbat. He works for Al-Sultan Saeed, and his most recent post was as commander of a ship in the Omani naval fleet bound for Mombasa and Zanzibar. None of this is news to them.

But now his visitors explain they are investigating the fate of the boy John Herman Paul who arrived in Yemen on the *Essex* a quarter of a century before, of whom no trace had been found. Abdullah fidgets, trying to pull up his wounded leg, which, after he has heard their words, seems to have acquired the weight of an anvil.

"If you are looking for John, I'm very sorry to tell you that you are too late ... much too late," Abdullah replies in a tone of pain and regret.

"Better late than never," the older man replies.

"Not in every case. Sometimes, not coming at all is better than coming late," Abdullah muses.

"She is still waiting for you!" The old man tosses the words out like a man laying his weapon down to be loaded, his eyes watching the mixed expressions passing across Abdullah's face. "She still leaves the door to your bedroom open, just as you asked her to do when you left, so that you won't wake her up if you return at night."

"What ... what? Who do you mean?" Abdullah feels an emptiness turn his insides upside down.

"You know very well who I mean," replies the man, staring directly into Abdullah's eyes.

"Things happen that cannot be undone. The book of life cannot be rewritten," Abdullah replies, as if trying to evade facing something.

"However regretful you are about your past, you can still write your own future," the man follows.

Abdullah mutters something unintelligible. He is now speaking to himself in a jumble of Arabic and English.

"Her hands are still stretched out to you, John!" the man finishes—words that Abdullah can't bear to hear.

"Who are you, sir? By God, tell me!" Abdullah asks in English, forcing himself to rise painfully from his seat.

"Don't you remember me, John? Have you forgotten your home in Salem?"

Abdullah examines the face of this old man, the whiteness of age covering his curved handlebar moustache.

"Could you be? No ... no ... you could not be my father."

"No, I am your neighbor, Clark. Your father passed away. You may remember how he repaired the roof of our house, not long before you left Salem."

Abdullah's eyes fill with tears. Standing before him is someone from his hometown of Salem. And who? A neighbor, a man he does not recognize.

"Yes, John. I'm sorry to tell you, your father died a long time ago. But your mother still sits on the porch of your home every day, watching for your return, as she's done ever since you left on the *Essex*."

The captain interjects. "Our ship will be sailing this afternoon, returning to Salem. Will you come with us?"

He is in no condition to respond, or even to think. It's as if time has stopped. He needs to catch his breath. Years come and go, a whole lifetime may go by, but when we think about those we love from afar, we hardly feel its passage.

The captain's voice startles him out of his trance, repeating his question: "Will you come on the ship?"

Abdullah thinks of his home in Mirbat, of Sayyida Khadija, Salma, and their twin sons, all waiting for him to return.

"You're too late, captain. You're too late, much too late."

The moment he speaks these words, he can no longer recall the image of his mother. It's as if her features have completely disappeared from his memory, evaporated from his mind, his worst fear come true at last.

The visitors continue trying to persuade him to embark with them but finally conclude they will not be able to sway him.

But before they take their leave, Abdullah asks them to wait a little. He has his assistant bring a box of his personal belongings, and from it takes a book. Handling it carefully, he wraps it in a muslin shirt for protection and presents it to the old man.

"This is the *Essex's* register. It also contains my story. I have kept a diary ever since the *Essex* left the shores of Massachusetts, until your visit this very day. Please give it to—" He pauses, his voice faltering as he tries to contain his emotions. "Please give it to my mother. Let her complete her part of the story." Their neighbor brings his face close to Abdullah's face and looks piercingly into his eyes.

"Why do you keep looking at me this way?" Abdullah asks, disconcerted.

"Because I know that your mother will do the same with me. She will read my eyes to verify that I actually saw you. Don't ask me how she does that."

The visitors depart for their ship, anchored in the port. Abdullah remains lying on his pallet as they disappear from view. *Somewhere in our lives, an ember burns; it may fade, even seem to disappear, but upon meeting someone it can return to life, making us grateful to those able to reignite the flame in our desolate souls.*

At the end of that day, Abdullah sits alone at the foot of the castle watching as a ship in the distance raises the American flag and sails southward, just as the setting sun disappears below the horizon over Africa. He hears someone playing a hushed tune on a flute and a castle worker singing. His words are lines from Jalal al-Din Rumi's poetry, his voice soft and mellow, as if steeped in agarwood oil mixed with the frankincense of Mirbat ...

> *I seek a chest tormented by parting*
> *To divulge the agony of longing.*
> *He who is cut off from his origin*
> *Longs for the moment of reunion.*

TIME: APRIL 2013

Place: Boston, Massachusetts

Tom finishes reading the translated ship's record and diary in disbelief. He looks around him and rubs his eyes, readjusting to his time and place. He feels like a time traveler just awakened from an incredible journey.

LOST SON OF SALEM: AN AMERICAN BOY'S ODYSSEY IN THE ARAB WORLD

He is now at the Starbucks in the departure lounge of Logan Airport in Boston. He has been sitting for two and a half hours, waiting for his flight to Los Angeles. He sips the last of his now-cold mocha, pondering the epic story behind it: the centuries-old chronicle of departure and discovery between the New World and the Old, a saga of colonization, trade, and wars, from the perilous times when men risked their lives in pursuit of Yemen's finest product to the unthinking moment it is served to him, topped with whipped cream.

This is the record of a life, not the record of a ship, Tom marvels to himself. It is most certainly a life record, the long and the short of it, the patience and the waiting, the yearning and the agony of separation, the desires of the heart, and the endless toil. It is closer to fantasy than reality, he thinks, like a story dreamed up by a Hollywood filmmaker. This story is particularly precious because he is one of the descendants, but—Tom's train of thought is interrupted by a strange notion. He pulls out the original book from its wooden box in his suitcase and looks at the date where it ends. Yes, there appear to be some pages missing—fallen out or possibly removed.

"One last thing ... the most important thing ..." Tom mutters to himself. He must know the end of the story. One essential question remains that has not been answered.

Did he ever meet her? Did he return to her? Was John, or Abdullah, or whatever his name was, destined to see his mother again? Or did she die before that was possible?"

He quickly searches the box, his heart beginning to race, in hopes of finding some hidden pages he hadn't noticed before. But he finds nothing. He slides his hands around the inside of the box, hoping to find some hidden pocket or cavity, to no avail. The last call to board his flight to Los Angeles blasts over the PA. He gathers his bag and the box and gets up to leave.

No, not to board his plane, but to go back to Salem. He will visit the grave of the woman he now understands to be John's mother, spend few extra days immersing himself in the place his people once knew. Casting a farewell look around the airport, he resolves that his next flight will be to Dhofar to search for the rest of the story ... that is, if anything remains.

The author can be reached at: comments.alfares@gmail.com

[1]A reference to the Hadith, "Heaven lies beneath mother's feet."